He ran a
keep you

I promise. Kelly brushed a lock of chestnut hair from his forehead, suddenly wanting to stay like this forever. Close to Dan. Sheltered from the rest of the world.

She met his gaze, the tension between them undeniable. She knew right then she wouldn't leave Summer Shores. Not until they'd seen their investigation through—together.

Without thinking, Kelly pressed her lips against his, gently at first, then hungrily. She needed the comfort of his touch, needed to lose herself with him, if only for a little while.

Dan's mouth moved to the soft flesh of her neck, his hands encircling her waist.

She wanted him. Wanted to feel his skin against hers, his hands on her body. More than anything, she longed to give herself to him completely.

Apprehension swelled in her gut. Her need was even more terrifying than the danger swirling around them....

Dear Harlequin Intrigue Reader,

You won't be able to resist a single one of our May books. We have a lineup so shiver inducing that you may forget summer's almost here!

- *Executive Bodyguard* is the second book in Debra Webb's exciting new trilogy, THE ENFORCERS. For the thrilling conclusion, be sure you pick up *Man of Her Dreams* in June.

- Amanda Stevens concludes her MATCHMAKERS UNDERGROUND series with *Matters of Seduction*. And the Montana McCalls are back, in B.J. Daniels's *Ambushed!*

- We also have two special premiers for you. Kathleen Long debuts in Harlequin Intrigue with *Silent Warning*, a chilling thriller. And LIPSTICK LTD., our special promotion featuring sexy, sassy sleuths, kicks off with Darlene Scalera's *Straight Silver*.

- A few of your favorite Harlequin Intrigue authors have some special books you'll love. Rita Herron's *A Breath Away* is available this month from HQN Books. And, in June, Joanna Wayne's *The Gentlemen's Club* is being published by Signature Spotlight.

Harlequin Intrigue brings you the best in breathtaking romantic suspense with six fabulous books to enjoy. Please write to us—we love to hear from our readers.

Sincerely,

Denise O'Sullivan
Senior Editor
Harlequin Intrigue

SILENT WARNING
KATHLEEN LONG

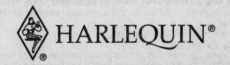

HARLEQUIN®

TORONTO • NEW YORK • LONDON
AMSTERDAM • PARIS • SYDNEY • HAMBURG
STOCKHOLM • ATHENS • TOKYO • MILAN • MADRID
PRAGUE • WARSAW • BUDAPEST • AUCKLAND

It's difficult to believe I'm sitting here typing the dedication for my first Harlequin Intrigue novel. Somebody pinch me.

I have so many people to thank—family, friends, writing buddies, mentors— all who believed this day would come. Thank you!

To Kim Nadelson, for giving me the opportunity of a lifetime, and to Paige Wheeler, for being a wonderful agent and cheerleader. Thank you both.

To my parents, who always taught me I could become whatever it was I dreamed of becoming. Thank you for the most important lesson of my life.

For my husband, Dan. I find it difficult to put into words how much your love and support mean to me. Thank you for standing beside me, supporting me as I worked to make my dream come true.

And last, but not least, for my father-in-law, Joseph Long. The world is a bit too quiet without you in it. We miss your smile and your stories. I'm quite sure you had a hand in this one, Dad. Thanks.

ISBN 0-373-22847-3

SILENT WARNING

Copyright © 2005 by Kathleen Long

This edition published by arrangement with Harlequin Books S.A.

® and TM are trademarks of the publisher. Trademarks indicated with ® are registered in the United States Patent and Trademark Office, the Canadian Trade Marks Office and in other countries.

www.eHarlequin.com

Printed in U.S.A.

ABOUT THE AUTHOR

Kathleen Long spent her career as a public relations consultant putting words into the mouths of others. In the summer of 2001, she decided it was time to put words into the mouths of her own fictional characters. She realized her dream of becoming a published author in early 2004 with her first sale.

Today she shares her life with her husband, Dan, and their neurotic sheltie. She divides her time between suburban Philadelphia and the New Jersey seashore, where she can often be found—hands on keyboard, bare toes in sand—spinning tales. After all, life doesn't get much better than that.

Please visit Kathleen at www.kathleenlong.com to say hello and take a peek at excerpts from upcoming releases.

CAST OF CHARACTERS

Rachel Braxton—Investigative reporter who drowns following an apparent drug overdose.

Kelly Weir—She travels to Summer Shores to pack up Rachel's belongings, but gets drawn in to the mystery surrounding her friend's death.

Dan Steele—He's convinced Rachel's death was no accident and is determined to uncover the killer's identity.

Diane Steele—Dan's younger sister also died of accidental drowning, with Oxygesic in her system.

Maddie Steele—Dan's mother may hold knowledge of the killer's identity locked in her dementia-damaged mind.

Jake Arnold—He's the local detective hesitant to believe Kelly and Dan's theories.

Helen Carroll—She's the feisty neighbor who befriends Kelly while keeping an eye out for trouble.

Vince Miller—He's the local pharmacist who may be doing a whole lot more than filling prescriptions.

Dr. Robinson—The primary physician at Serenity Pain Institute—is he hiding valuable information?

Scott Jansen—He's the State Pharmacy Board employee quite certain something illegal is brewing in Summer Shores.

Jim Braxton—Rachel's brother is counting on Kelly to handle the details of his sister's affairs.

Jane Weir—Kelly's sister calls with news of a crucial clue.

Rick DeSanto—He's a reporter from Kelly's hometown who provides information on Miller's past.

Frank and Marge Healey—They're nosy locals who provide a bit of insight into Rachel's life.

Prologue

He dug his fingers into the flesh of her upper arm, relishing the lack of resistance beneath his grip.

"You're hurting me." Rachel Braxton's words were nothing more than a whimper. Probably all the so-called reporter could manage. Typical.

He raised a brow then yanked her forward, the dense foliage snapping as he pulled her through. A tangle of weeds raked her bare legs and she stumbled, letting out another cry.

Weak. So weak.

A trickle of blood trailed the length of her shin, mesmerizing him for a moment. It was a shame to mar her beautiful body, but she'd left him no choice.

He refocused on his task, dragging her behind him. He ducked beneath a large branch, laughing as it caught her in the face, clawing her neck and hooking the chain of her locket.

She groped for the necklace too late and it was gone, vanishing into the dark depths of the marsh.

"My necklace."

Her whine turned his stomach. As if she didn't

have bigger things to worry about. "You won't need it where you're going."

"Let me go." Terror tinged her voice. Good. It was about time. "I don't have what you need, but I'll help you. I'll do whatever I can. I swear."

He stopped then, savoring the fear glistening in her brown gaze. "Should have thought of that a long time ago, sweetheart."

Her expression pleaded with him, anxious and begging. Too little. Too late.

"I'm telling you the truth," she whispered, a tear sliding over her lower lid.

"Honey, you haven't told me the truth since the day we met." He smiled, enjoying the widening of her eyes, the shortness of her breath. The hunted and the hunter. Her desperation and his power.

He jerked her into motion, excitement slithering through him as they reached the edge of the trees. The glistening water of the sound appeared as they broke through to the clearing. Pale moonlight dappled the surface like a ghostly dance of lost souls. Perfect.

A small boat sat anchored next to the marshy beach. He shoved her forward. "Get in."

"No." Rachel stiffened as if steeling herself in one last desperate effort to appear fearless.

He leveled his gun at her face. "Now."

Her body sagged as she climbed into the boat and dropped onto the unforgiving bench. Her teeth chattered noisily. She wrapped her arms around her waist as he pushed the boat from the shore, the small vessel slipping like a whisper through the murky water.

When they neared the inlet, he started the motor, raising his gaze to meet her terrified stare. "Enjoying your ride?"

Her trembling intensified. She lowered her head, her long blond hair covering her face as she gagged, vomiting onto the floor of his boat. The acrid smell mixed with the damp, salt air. He winced. *So weak.* Useless, actually. It was unfortunate. With her brains and investigative skills, she could have accomplished great things.

He kicked her foot, grinning as she looked up. "Chin up. You're about to get the story of your life."

He watched as her eyes darkened, the reality of her fate settling upon her. She lowered her head again, this time to pray, her words whispering into the unforgiving night.

"God, please help me...."

Too bad he didn't have his camera. She'd be one to immortalize. One more example of how untouchable he was.

She'd thought she could expose him, but he was about to prove her wrong.

Dead wrong.

He laughed, throwing back his head to let his laughter mingle with the sound of her prayer.

Chapter One

Kelly Weir shifted her Jetta into Park, staring up through the windshield at the gray bungalow. Cool, autumn air whipped through the sunroof, surrounding her with the smell of salt air and sunshine. She snapped off the volume on the radio then cut the car's ignition.

It had been less than twenty-four hours since Rachel's brother, Jim, had called, yet here she was in Summer Shores, North Carolina. Her agreement to help the family by packing up Rachel's things had been a knee-jerk reaction, the news of Rachel's death having rocked her to the core.

Scrutinizing the weathered lines of the small house, she blew out a slow breath and tamped down the sadness lurking at the back of her brain. How long had it been since she and Rachel had spoken? More than a year?

Kelly climbed from the car, popped the trunk and threw her backpack over her shoulder. Time to get this over with. She grabbed two other bags and headed for the stairs, the distressed wood creaking beneath her as she climbed toward a screened-in porch.

She dropped one of her bags onto the painted decking, shifting to reach the key she'd shoved in her pocket. Her elbow brushed against the front door and it cracked open. Kelly's pulse quickened. She narrowed her eyes suspiciously, pushing the door open wide to glance inside.

The floors and furniture gleamed, an orange scent heavy in the air. Jim had mentioned there might be housecleaners here when she arrived. Judging by the appearance of the place, she'd just missed them, and they'd obviously forgotten to lock up.

Breathing a sigh of relief, she stepped inside, lowering her bags to the floor. She tossed her backpack onto a faded teal sofa and crossed to the kitchen window to let in some additional fresh air.

She'd no sooner slid up the old wooden sash than a noise sounded from another part of the house. Kelly stopped short, anxiety whispering through her.

Her imagination. It had been a long day and her mind must be playing tricks on her. She gazed out the window, trying to focus on the scent of brine hanging on the ocean breeze.

Thump.

A chill rippled down her spine. Darn it. She wasn't *that* tired.

She steadied herself, trying to think rationally. The sun was out. People didn't rob houses in broad daylight, did they? It was probably a neighbor doing something…neighborly. Surely everyone knew of

Rachel's death by now. Maybe someone had stopped by to help pack her things.

Better still, maybe a window was loose, or a door or something. This was Summer Shores, North Carolina after all. Small town. Friendly. Safe. There were a multitude of possibilities for why the house was making a—

Thump.

Her nervous gaze landed on a spiral staircase that dropped to the lower level just past the main section of the living room. Whatever—or whoever—was making the noise was downstairs.

The small hairs at the nape of Kelly's neck pricked to attention.

Eyeing a pair of pewter candlesticks, she tiptoed across the floor to grasp one, the metal cold and heavy in her now-shaking hand.

Thump.

She started, white-knuckling the candlestick and holding it high. "Who's there?" She forced out her voice, strong and loud. Not bad for being completely rattled. Not bad at all.

Keeping the candlestick between herself and the stairs, she fumbled in her backpack for her cell phone, pulling it free and pressing the Power button.

She moved toward the front door, planning to get out before anyone could answer.

The noise from below had stopped. Probably a stray animal or something completely harmless, but she wasn't taking any chances. She backed toward the door, trying to punch 911 on the tiny keypad. Darn these things.

"Whoever you are," she yelled. "I'm calling the police."

"I assure you I'm harmless," a man's voice answered.

The deep timbre sent awareness and fear washing through Kelly. She stumbled and the candlestick fell from her grasp, clattering loudly against the wood floor.

A dark-haired man appeared at the top of the steps, raising both hands in a gesture of surrender. "Didn't mean to frighten you." His midnight-blue gaze moved from Kelly to the candlestick to Kelly again. One dark brow arched. "Were you planning to use that on me?"

Kelly picked up the heavy metal object, pointing it at him. Her heart jackhammered in her chest. "Who are you?"

"I'm a…was…a friend of Rachel's." His expression softened, but the furrow between his brows remained. Deep lines etched into his forehead, leaving no doubt he was a man on a mission. "She had something of mine and I thought I'd pick it up before you got here."

Kelly blinked, her head spinning from the surge of adrenaline racing through her. The man took a step forward and her breath caught. His well-worn denim shirt stretched taut across broad shoulders, his stance conveying nothing but sureness and pure male virility. Her heart slapped so loudly against her ribs, she had no doubt he could hear her fright.

She glanced at the cell phone in her hand. "How do I know you're telling the truth? I should call the police."

"The name's Dan Steele." He continued toward her, close-cropped chestnut-brown hair framing his rugged, thirtysomething face. "They know me."

"Oh. This is a frequent activity of yours?" Kelly backed onto the porch and punched the last digit into the phone. "Don't push your luck."

"I'm telling the truth. Here." Steele dangled a small silver object toward her. "She'd given me a key."

Kelly suddenly felt like an idiot. She knew nothing about Rachel's recent life. This guy might have been her lover for all she knew.

She concentrated on calming her whirling mind. "How did you know her?"

"Friend," he repeated.

"And what did you need?"

He hesitated, reawakening her suspicions. "Something."

"Something?" She frowned. "How do I know you're not a fast-talking burglar?"

"With a key?" He shook his head, his expression incredulous.

"You never know." Kelly set the candlestick on the floor and held out her open palm, nodding toward the key. "I'll take that. I'd rather not have you stopping back unexpectedly. Nothing personal."

One dark brow arched again as Steele pressed the key into her hand, his touch lingering a moment too long. Heat built at the spot where their skin met, searing her palm. The man's intense stare never left hers, and Kelly fought the urge to look away. She had no intention of giving him the satisfaction.

"Just what is it you're missing?" she asked as she closed her fingers around his key then pocketed it, still gripping the cell phone tightly in her other hand.

"You know, you look a bit like her around the—"

"I know." Kelly pinned him with a glare, frustration edging out her fear. "Don't change the subject."

"I'm leaving now." He brushed past her and pushed the screen door open.

"I have half a mind to check out your story," she called after him as he headed toward the steps.

He stopped short, turning to face her, his smile not quite reaching his deep blue eyes. "This didn't go well. I'll stop back later."

Kelly focused on drawing deep slow breaths as she watched him cross the drive. The air seemed to still, as if the man owned the space around him and the ground beneath his confident stride. He turned toward the beach without looking back. Much to her dismay, a purely female response tangled with the anger and fear battling within her. The man oozed vitality—raw, male and intriguing.

She shivered with awareness.

He no doubt had known Rachel. Kelly's friend had been beautiful, and never had trouble turning a male head. Dan Steele apparently had not been immune to her charms.

When he was fully out of sight, Kelly dropped her cell phone into her bag and headed for the kitchen. She plucked the receiver from the wall phone, dialing the keypad—911.

Hers might not be a true emergency, but if Steele

planned to follow through on his promise to return,
she intended to find out exactly who he was.

DAN STOOD AND STARED at the ocean. The woman had
unnerved him. There weren't many things in his life
capable of eliciting that response. Not anymore.

He should have headed out the side door instead of
checking the third bedroom. There'd been nothing
there. He'd managed only to wedge his arm behind a
bookcase reaching for a blank sheet of paper. As if
Rachel would be that careless with anything important.

Rubbing a hand across his eyes, he headed up the
beach toward his house, the woman's face filling his
mind. At first it had been like looking at a ghost, but
once her fiery spirit flashed through her mesmerizing deep brown gaze, he knew she was no Rachel.
Rachel had always put on a good show, but behind
her reporter's notebook, she was nothing more than
a pretty bundle of nerves.

The friend had hidden her fear and surprise admi-
rably. Beauty and backbone. Imagine. A longing
stirred deep within him—evidence he wasn't completely dead inside after all. No matter. He needed
to find Rachel's notes, not worry about her friend.

His interest in Rachel's work had been personal.
During his tenure in pharmaceutical marketing, his
pet project had been one drug in particular. Oxygesic. Its development had been a godsend for those
suffering from chronic pain and cancer. Then people began to die from its misuse.

People like Diane. His baby sister.

The familiar ache squeezed his heart, but he shoved it away, digging deep for the determination that had carried him this far.

Now that Rachel's notes had apparently gone missing, Dan was even more convinced her death was no accident. She'd been the only person to listen to his theories. His gut told him she'd uncovered something someone hadn't wanted her to find. The frantic message she'd left for him the day she disappeared confirmed as much.

And now she was dead.

He cast a glance toward the ocean, watching the September swells crash against the deserted beach, swirling against each other before they slid back out to sea. Riptide. Opposing currents. The story of his life.

His cell phone chirped to life, yanking him from his thoughts. "Yes."

"Who the hell do you think you are now? The damned welcoming committee?" Detective Jake Arnold's voice barked in his ear. Dan winced, the annoyance palpable in his old friend's tone. "Meet me at your house. Ten minutes."

The phone clicked dead.

Great. As if he needed any more complications today.

KELLY REPLACED the receiver and headed for the lower level of the house. Her call to the sheriff's office had gotten her nowhere other than having to listen to Dan Steele's upstanding citizen résumé. Apparently he'd settled here a few years ago, returning to his roots after a successful career up North.

She hadn't been able to glean much more in the way of detail, but the tone of the woman she'd spoken to had made it clear he was one of Summer Shores' favorite sons. What did Kelly expect? Small towns protected their own.

A light glowed from a spare bedroom as she rounded the bottom of the steps. Nothing seemed out of place as she peered inside, but then, she'd never set eyes on the house before today. Kelly opened each drawer and ran her hand over both shelves in the closet. Nothing. She sank onto the edge of the bed.

What had he been looking for?

Exhaustion washed over her, the earlier adrenaline fading from her system. She fingered the corner of a letter she'd tucked into her sweatshirt pocket as the numbing reality of Rachel's death uncoiled from the pit of her stomach.

How many other letters and phone calls from Rachel had she ignored over the past year? Dozens? Yet, this one had been different. In it, Rachel had begged for forgiveness. Begged. But Kelly had ignored her plea, clinging instead to the grudge she'd carried instead of making amends. Now Rachel was dead. Drowned in the ocean she'd loved.

An inexplicable sense of dread sent a shudder down Kelly's spine. Hoping she'd find some coffee to help erase the chill, she headed back toward the stairs, looking up just as she rounded the bottom step.

Her heart slammed into her ribs.

A large, gray tomcat loomed at the top of the steps, two yellow eyes lazily winking down at her.

"Who are you?" She was beginning to think that was the question of the day. Did everybody have a key?

The cat rose to his paws and stretched, leaning into the side of her leg as she passed.

"Edgar," a female voice called from outside.

Kelly squinted at the cat, which still studied her curiously. "Edgar?" He rubbed against her calf, stretched then kicked out his back feet as he headed toward the door.

Opening the door to step onto the porch, Kelly let the cat saunter ahead. An elderly woman toting a large bakery box looked up from the bushes along the driveway.

"Are you looking for your cat?" Kelly asked.

The woman's gaze narrowed as she spotted Edgar sitting at the screen door. "Oh, that bum. Was he bothering you?"

"Not at all."

"You the friend from up North?" The woman walked to the bottom of the steps, the bakery box nestled in the crook of her arm, a lit cigarette dangling from the opposite hand. She paused to take a drag.

"Kelly Weir."

"I'm Helen Carroll." She waved the glowing butt over her shoulder. "Live across the street. Heard you were coming and thought you could use a welcome." She waved the cigarette toward the cat. "Guess he thought the same thing."

"No problem. Would you like to come up?"

"Thanks." Helen dropped the cigarette and ground

it out with the toe of a red high-top sneaker. A Surf Naked sweatshirt topped a pair of faded, black jeans. Wild spikes of snow-white hair framed her tanned, weathered face. She climbed the wooden steps with the nimbleness of a teenager, balancing the box in one arm and skimming the railing with the other. Her eyes remained lowered, focused on the steps. "I brought you some cinnamon buns. Figured you could use something sweet after your drive."

"Thank you."

"It's a small town. We try to be neighborly."

"So I've heard," Kelly muttered under her breath.

As she reached the top of the steps, the woman raised her pale gaze to look at Kelly. "I'll be darned." Her features fell slack. "You look just like her."

"Everyone always thought we were sisters."

Helen slowly shook her head, staring intently at Kelly's features.

"You're the one who found her, aren't you?" Sadness flickered through Kelly as she spoke the words.

Helen sighed, handing her the pastry box. "I'd like to forget that day. Haven't walked on the beach since."

"I'm sorry."

"Well, I'm sorry about your friend."

"Actually—" Kelly took the box, doing her best to focus on the printed logo rather than the regret building inside her "—we hadn't spoken in a long time."

"She told me." Helen ran a hand through the front of her hair, a kind smile spreading across her face. "We'd talk sometimes."

"Did you know her well?"

The woman shrugged. "I don't think anybody knew her well. She was always out looking for a story."

Kelly warmed, remembering Rachel's tenacity. "Her specialty."

"Hadn't seen her in a while. Figured she had a hot one cooking." A shadow passed across Helen's face. She glanced down at her feet then up at Kelly, her lips parting as if she were about to speak. After a moment, she shook her head, apparently dismissing whatever it had been that had crossed her mind.

She turned back toward the steps. "I'm sure you've got plenty to do to get settled in, and I'm missing my shows. Holler if you need anything. I'm across the way in the little gray shack."

"Thanks." Kelly held the door as Helen stepped outside. "Want a sticky bun for the road?"

The slender woman shook her head as she descended the steps and started across the driveway.

"Do you know a man named Dan Steele?" Kelly blurted out the question before the woman was out of earshot.

Helen stopped short and turned, her eyes wide. "You meet him?"

"He was downstairs when I got here. Did he know Rachel?"

"That he did." Helen thought for a moment, then grinned. "Got a nice caboose, that one."

Kelly stood, stunned, watching the woman and her cat cross the street. *A nice caboose?*

The man's handsome features flashed through her mind, and she fought back her quickening pulse.

Doing her best to ignore the attraction thrumming through her veins, she pulled open the screen door and slipped into the house. She had work to do.

DETECTIVE JAKE ARNOLD steepled his fingers and leaned across Dan's kitchen table. "Want to tell me what you were doing in Rachel's house?"

"I forgot some socks." Dan shot an impatient glare at his friend. He didn't have time for a full inquisition. The sooner he could send Jake on his way, the better.

"Right." Jake's blond brows snapped together. "So why didn't you tell our newest visitor that? Might have saved us all a lot of trouble."

Dan shrugged, not answering.

Jake leaned back, lacing his fingers behind his head. "I'll tell you why. You refuse to accept Rachel died accidentally, isn't that right?"

Dan remained silent, doing his best to keep his face emotionless.

Jake nodded toward the glass sliders and the roaring ocean outside. "Hell of a riptide out there this time of year. People swim alone. Sometimes they drown." He pursed his lips, stood and took a step toward Dan. "Forget Rachel Braxton and leave this friend of hers alone."

Dan straightened, growing annoyed at Jake's condescending attitude. He plucked a photograph from the stone mantel. "Her investigation had to do with Diane." He thrust the frame toward Jake.

Jake narrowed his gaze, his jaw stiffening. He took the frame, touching a finger to the image beneath the glass. "I loved your sister." He met Dan's stare, the edge gone from his blue eyes. "But she did something stupid and she died. It was an accident."

Frustration and anger eased through Dan. "She'd never use drugs. You know that."

"What about a drug her own brother helped bring to market?" Jake leaned forward, brows furrowed. "Maybe she wouldn't think twice." He set the framed picture back on the mantel, turning for the front door. "Stay away from the whole Rachel Braxton thing."

"It wasn't an accident."

"The subject's closed." Jake yanked open the door, casting a warning glance in Dan's direction. "I may be your friend, but I won't hesitate to toss you in jail if you break into that house again."

The door slammed closed behind him.

Dan crossed to the sliding glass door, stopping to stare out at the churning ocean. Rachel had found some proof of illegal activity involving Oxygesic, and whatever she'd found would lead him to the truth behind his sister's death. He knew it in his gut.

But where were her notes? They had to be somewhere in that house—somewhere he hadn't thought of before her friend had interrupted.

Jake could toss out all the threats he wanted. Dan had every intention of getting back inside Rachel's house.

KELLY CARRIED the box of sticky buns into the kitchen and pushed it to the back of the counter. She found a half-empty tin of coffee in the freezer, started the coffeemaker then decided to check the rest of the house.

A narrow hallway led to two bedrooms and a bath. French doors opened from the larger room to the back deck. Beyond the faded gray railing, the water of the sound sparkled.

Inside, a spotless mahogany desk took up a third of the room; a printer and fax sitting next to a gleaming desktop computer. Rachel's pride and joy. Her writing.

At least the equipment would make managing Kelly's clients easier while she was here. After all, she didn't have to be in Philadelphia to meet graphic design deadlines.

A photograph on the nightstand caught her attention as she turned back toward the kitchen. In it, she and Rachel smiled brightly, kneeling on top of Jockey's Ridge. Beach week in the Outer Banks of North Carolina.

Rachel's blond hair blew around her face to mingle with strands of Kelly's auburn waves. Brilliant periwinkle and fuchsia ribbons of sky framed their suntanned faces, the sun only partially visible behind the huge sand dune. Identical wide-spaced brown eyes sparkled in both faces.

Frick and Frack. They'd been inseparable since first grade. Kelly's parents had been more concerned about their tee times at the country club than they'd been about their daughter. Her friendship with Rachel had been her one true source of solace.

She had thought they'd be friends forever, until Rachel had used a bogus scandal involving Kelly as fodder for a front-page story. Kelly touched her fingertips to the glass covering the photo. Smooth. Cold. Lifeless.

A long while later, after she'd unpacked and settled in, she lay in Rachel's bed staring into the darkness. Dan Steele's rugged features popped into her mind uninvited. She shoved the image away, ignoring the curiosity simmering in her belly. There was no sense in thinking about the handsome stranger or whatever he'd been looking for.

Tomorrow she'd pack up Rachel's things and be gone. The friendship she and Rachel had once shared was lost forever. As much as she longed for closure, she'd never find it at the bottom of a packing box.

THE BEDSPREAD rose and fell with each breath the woman took. A sliver of pale moonlight shimmered through the door, lighting her face.

She looked so much like Rachel he felt a chill. He'd heard the murmuring around town and had wanted to see for himself. Not that he cared. Not really. As long as she packed up Rachel's things and left, he didn't care if she was the dead woman's spitting image.

He pulled a hard candy from his pocket, peeling the wrapper as quietly as he could. He slipped the morsel between his lips, grimacing. Grape. He was growing tired of grape.

He watched the woman for a few more minutes before he turned and walked down the hall, stopping in the kitchen to throw out the wrapper, not caring if she noticed.

He only cared that this one didn't cause trouble. Not now.

He balled his hands into fists. If she did stick her nose where it didn't belong, she'd end up just like her little friend.

Very wet. And very dead.

Chapter Two

Kelly woke to the sensation of weight at the end of the bed. Something moved alongside her and she struggled to open her eyes. A large gray face purred like an engine, nuzzling her cheek.

Her stomach pitched with the sudden contact and awakening. "Edgar. You scared me half to death."

She gave him a quick pat on the head and threw off the covers. Grabbing her sweatshirt from the back of the chair, she pulled it over her nightshirt.

"Come on. Let's figure out how you got in."

The front door remained closed, locked as she'd left it. As she checked the doorknob, Edgar walked into the kitchen and let out a meow.

"I don't have anything for you, baby. Sorry. I'll get you some tuna when I hit the grocery store."

Kelly trotted down the spiral steps to the lower level. The inner door sat ajar, a sliver of daylight glowing brightly between the wood and the frame.

"Great." She rubbed her tired eyes. In her exhaustion the night before, she'd never thought to check downstairs when she locked up. "Good thing I'm not at home. The axe murderer would have walked right in."

Edgar pushed past her, nudging the screen door open. He slipped through, stretching out his back legs before he swaggered down the walk.

Kelly pulled both doors tight and flipped the dead bolt. She trudged up the stairs, deciding Edgar had the right idea. Food was a definite priority.

Twenty minutes later, she'd dressed and headed south toward the shopping area she remembered from her college days. When a supermarket appeared, she zipped into the lot, quickly parking her car and pulling a shopping cart from the cue.

The grocery store was deserted except for a group of senior citizens gathered in the produce section. She supposed everything slowed down once mid-September arrived and tourist season ended.

Scanning each aisle, Kelly tossed only essentials into her cart, choosing just enough to hold her for a day or two. She had no intention of staying in this small town any longer than that.

An end cap piled high with freshly baked chocolate chip cookies beckoned to her. Why not? She reached to pluck a plastic container from the display, starting when a slender hand touched her arm.

"Why are you here?" An elderly woman eyed her quizzically. Short white hair waved gently around her face, her cloudy blue eyes blinking then refocusing on Kelly.

"Pardon me?" Kelly took a step back, thrown off balance by the encounter.

"You don't belong here. You're dead."

Adrenaline spiked in Kelly's veins. She pulled her arm from the woman's grasp.

"He killed you." The woman's voice dropped to a whisper. "I saw him."

"Maddie," a voice called out. "Let's get you back with the group."

A young woman sporting wire-rimmed glasses smiled at Kelly, gently taking the woman by the elbow. "I'm sorry. Sometimes she gets confused during our outings."

Kelly shook her head. "No problem." Was it a case of confusion? Or had the woman mistaken her for Rachel? Heaven knew, it had been happening for years.

Maddie shrugged off the younger woman's touch, pointing a bony finger at Kelly.

"He killed you." Her soft voice sent tremors through Kelly's bones. "The Candy Man killed you."

The young woman shook her head, smiling nervously. "I'm very sorry." She put her arm around Maddie, this time leading her away.

Frozen to the spot, Kelly watched as the old woman turned to waggle a finger in her direction. Kelly's pulse and thoughts raced at matched speeds. What on earth had just happened? And what had the woman meant?

Rachel had drowned. Right?

Shaking off the encounter as just what the younger woman had said, she turned her attention back to her cart.

The sooner she paid and left, the sooner she'd be able to start packing up Rachel's things.

DAN SIGHED deeply, rubbing his tired eyes. He scribbled another note onto the pad of paper then scratched a line through the words.

No matter what scenario he used, no matter what theory he tried, the puzzle came back to Rachel. She'd believed something illegal was going on in Summer Shores and had done nothing but gather information during the last weeks of her life. He'd encouraged her every step of the way, urging her to dig deeper.

And now she was dead.

Guilt and doubt tangled inside him. If only he'd been there to take her call. Could he have saved her somehow? He stretched his neck, willing his frustrated brain to work through the mystery of what had happened.

Where were her notes?

He spun his chair to face a wall of framed photos, focusing on his favorite. Diane proudly held a huge bluefish at arm's length as their mother looked on. Broad grins illuminated both faces.

Dan plucked his coffee mug from the desk and took a long swallow.

His mother and sister. He'd lost them both in a manner of speaking. Diane had drowned two weeks after the picture had been taken. His mother's mini strokes and her downward spiral into dementia had landed her in the nursing home three months later.

Perhaps fate had taken away his mother's ability to remember Diane's inexplicable death, but it hadn't taken away the thoughts that haunted Dan.

Even though his father had deserted them when

he and his sister were young, his mother had never remarried, never loved again. Her obvious heartache had taught him to focus on career, not family. Yet now he found himself faced with a grim reality. His sister was dead because of a drug he'd brought to market, and the vital mother he'd once known was fading away. He'd never be able to recapture the years he'd lost with both.

Dan knew in his heart Diane's death had been no accident—just as Rachel's had been no accident. He'd have no peace until he found the truth. All he had to do was piece together the facts—if only he could find them.

Narrowing his focus, he made another notation on the pad, this time circling his writing. He might not have Rachel's notes to work with, but he had her house—and her friend.

THE MORNING had brightened by the time Kelly finished unpacking the groceries. She poured a fresh cup of coffee and headed for Rachel's work area, banishing all thoughts of her unsettling grocery store trip to the recesses of her brain.

She walked into the bedroom and sat her mug on Rachel's desk. Pulling open the French doors to let in the autumn breeze, she inhaled the moist air, pungent with the scent of the bay and marsh grasses. She tipped her face to the sun, letting the warmth permeate her skin.

How sad that Rachel would never feel the sun's warmth or the brush of a damp sea breeze against her face again. Why had Kelly been so stubborn about a reconciliation? Oh, who was she kidding? She'd learned from the best. Her parents had taken every grudge they'd ever held to their graves.

She forced herself to concentrate on Rachel's desk. Maybe taking care of the loose ends would help ease the guilt in her heart.

Kelly sank into the chair and pulled open the file drawer. Neatly labeled colored folders lined the hanging file frame. Rachel had always had an amazing work ethic—driven to the brink of obsession, actually. Had it gotten her killed?

No. Kelly shook her head. That thought came solely from the ramblings of the woman in the grocery store. Her words had no basis in reality.

Refocusing her attention, Kelly pulled a file labeled Outstanding Queries and spread it open on the desk. In alphabetical order by target market, the letters ranged from one for *Family Circle* to one for the *Washington Post*.

Kelly turned back to the drawer, fingering through the remaining folders. Working articles. Someone needed to tell these editors their articles weren't going to make deadline.

One by one, Kelly pulled each contact number and placed the call. An hour later she was done, returning each folder to its place in the drawer.

A knock sounded at the front door and she jumped, her stomach tilting sideways. *Chicken.* The woman in the grocery store had made more of an impression than she cared to admit.

She padded down the hall and pulled open the inner door. Dan Steele stood on the other side of the locked screen door, leaning against the doorjamb, the sharp line of his jaw set with even more intensity than it had been the day before. Shadows tinged the skin beneath his eyes, but the blue heat of his gaze coiled Kelly's stomach into a tight knot.

"You again." She frowned.

He held up his hands. "Let's start over."

She narrowed her eyes.

He swept one arm in a grand gesture. "Welcome to North Carolina."

Kelly glared at him, not sure how to answer his statement. "Back for another look?"

His features tensed, his expression growing serious. "Actually, yes."

"Forget it." Kelly moved to close the door.

Dan leaned his forehead against the screen. He might look like an expectant child with his face plastered against an ice-cream parlor window, but Kelly knew better.

"It's imperative I explain something to you about Rachel."

Kelly eyed him carefully, her curiosity getting the best of her. "Like what?"

"Let me in and I'll tell you."

"I can hear you just fine through that locked door."

She met his stare, angling her chin determinedly.

"Fair enough." He straightened.

He stood easily taller than six feet, his presence commanding. His brown hair tumbled carelessly, as if he had just run a strong hand through the short strands. Kelly's gaze followed the drape of his navy sweatshirt to the trim fit of his khaki shorts. Her pulse quickened at the sight of his bare, muscular legs. One thing was for certain. The man was in some serious physical shape.

The breeze picked up, washing Dan's clean scent past her into the house. Every one of Kelly's nerve endings snapped to attention. She hugged herself, glad to have the door between her stirring attraction and the man who'd inspired the unwanted response.

The last man who'd evoked such a visceral reaction had turned out to be anything but what he'd first seemed. She had no intention of repeating the mistake.

"I need you to listen carefully."

The ferocity of Dan's gaze startled her, capturing her full attention. "I'm listening."

"I met Rachel when she interviewed me about my sister."

"Your sister?"

Dan nodded. "She died of a drug overdose last year, and Rachel was doing a piece on the same drug. Oxygesic."

A momentary shadow passed across his face, but he continued, "My sister was an athlete. She'd never take that drug knowingly."

Kelly said nothing, riveted by the man on the other side of the door.

"I need Rachel's notes." He stepped close to the screen, erasing any space between them. "You need to let me search this house."

She considered his request, scouring his face for any sign he might be lying. She found none. "I already went through her files."

Dan's eyes widened.

Kelly shook her head. "I'm sorry, but there's nothing on Oxy…Oxy…"

"Oxygesic." Disappointment darkened his gaze. "That makes no sense. A friend of hers died high on the stuff. Crashed a car into a pole. Rachel was obsessed with that story."

"What kind of drug is it?"

Hope flickered across his features. "A time-released opiate."

"Opiate?"

"Painkiller."

Kelly blinked, confused. "Did her friend take too many?"

"Maybe not." Dan stared deeply into her eyes, sending a jolt of electricity straight to her core. "Sometimes it only takes one."

Kelly took a step back, wanting to put a bit of distance between her and this man's determination. "Is it a controlled substance?"

He nodded, his expression grim. "It's not difficult to get illegally, unfortunately."

"How?"

"Sometimes it's a crooked doctor writing phony prescriptions." Anger flashed through his eyes. "Sometimes it's a crooked pharmacist."

It was evident Dan had decided on the latter. "You think it's a pharmacist?"

"Guy named Miller."

"How would he get away with it?"

His voice dropped low, intense. "That's what I need to find out."

Thoughts and questions raced through Kelly's

mind. "I'm still not understanding how this drug can kill someone unless they take too many."

Dan's gaze wavered momentarily as if he wasn't quite ready to answer her question. When he spoke again, he did so slowly.

"The drug is time-released, meant to be swallowed. If you chew the tablet, you experience a rush. Some people stop breathing."

"Like your sister?"

"Supposedly. The coroner said her heart failed while she was swimming. The Oxygesic was already in her system."

"And you don't believe it?"

"Call it a brother's hunch, but no." His gaze roamed her face, trailing hot paths across her skin as if he were searching for a sign she believed him. "Rachel left a message on my machine saying she'd found something unbelievable. She didn't want to talk on the phone. I never heard from her again."

Kelly's breath caught. "You believe Rachel's death had something to do with the story?"

He nodded, the muscles of his jaw clenching tight.

They stood in silence for several long moments, eyes locked. Kelly fought the urge to look away, entranced by the depth of emotion evident in Dan's gaze.

What if he was right? Didn't Rachel deserve for the truth to be uncovered? No matter what had happened between them, if Kelly had been the one who died, Rachel would have left no stone unturned in her quest for the truth.

Kelly scrutinized the man before her, realizing

she'd never seen anyone more sure of what he believed. Unlatching the screen door, she pushed it open. "Maybe I missed something. Why don't we look together?"

A few moments later, Dan patted the computer monitor in Rachel's bedroom. "Did you check this?" He squinted, his suntanned skin crinkling into fine lines around his eyes.

Kelly dragged her attention from his appealing features to the computer. "Not yet. I've only been through her filing cabinet."

She sank into the chair as Dan powered on the machine. A welcome screen flashed a box for password entry.

"Any ideas?" Dan leaned close. Kelly stole a glance at the strong angular lines of his profile, mentally chastising herself. So the guy had a good story; the reality was she didn't know him from Adam.

"Actually, yes." She typed in a single word. *Nellie.*

The screen instantly displayed the operating system's start up page.

"Nellie?" Incredulity tinged Dan's tone.

"Nellie Bly. First woman reporter," Kelly explained. "Rachel's idol." *And one heck of a lucky guess.*

Within seconds they both stared at the screen, scanning the list of files on Rachel's system. Kelly was just losing hope when her gaze landed on two words. *Black market.*

"Whoa." Dan spoke at the same instant. "That has to be it."

DAN WATCHED as Kelly scrolled back, double-clicking the title. He held his breath as the document opened, trying to ignore the creamy expanse of her neck just inches away. She'd swept her long, auburn hair up into some sort of clip, and if he weren't so intent on finding Rachel's notes, he might find the sight distracting.

Okay. Truth was, the woman was very distracting, but he'd promised himself a long time ago to avoid matters of the heart. He'd listened to his mother cry behind her closed bedroom door enough to know true love was nothing more than a myth. Besides, all he cared about right now were the words on the screen.

"Frank Jones. *Virginian-Pilot,*" Kelly read out loud, curiosity palpable in her voice as she skimmed the query letter. "I didn't find an acceptance letter for this one." She twisted in the chair, her rich brown gaze jolting Dan's senses. "Maybe she never got the assignment."

"Or maybe someone got to her notes but not to her computer files." Satisfaction filled him. He'd been right all along.

Kelly dialed Information then rang the newspaper's switchboard. She whispered she'd been put into Frank Jones's voice mail as she listened.

"All we can do is wait." Dan shrugged a few moments later as she set the receiver back in its cradle.

The phone rang within seconds, the shrill ring startling them both. Hope uncoiled in Dan's gut.

Kelly answered the call then frowned. "My sister," she mouthed.

Disappointment washed through him as he moved

away to give her space. No matter. Sooner or later, Jones would return their call, and he'd be one step closer to the truth.

He watched a myriad of expressions play across Kelly's face as she spoke to her sister.

"Open it," she said, her features growing tense. She shot him a confused look and his breath caught at the uncertainty in her gaze.

She'd been nothing but cool since the moment she'd first found him in the house, but right now, at this moment, a glimpse of the vulnerable woman within shone through.

"A post office key?" Kelly's voice grew tight, climbing up at least two octaves. "She didn't enclose any sort of note?"

He watched as her frown deepened the soft lines that framed her wide-spaced brown eyes. There was an intensity to the woman that intrigued him, a hint of a past pain or secret she kept carefully tucked away.

She hung up the phone and dragged a hand through her hair.

Concern eased through him, and he stepped close. "You all right?"

Kelly visibly started, as if the question had taken her by surprise. She nodded. "Rachel sent me a post office key. My sister's overnighting it down."

KELLY COULDN'T HELP but admire the light that sparked to life in Dan's vibrant, blue stare when she explained her sister's call. His intensity and determination were characteristics to admire, and to watch.

Her ex-fiancé had taught her all about driven

men—ones who stopped at nothing to get their way. Was Dan Steele cut from the same cloth?

He stood close, leaning his full weight against the desktop, eyes wide. "Let's hope it yields her notes." He straightened his features, as if consciously working to hide his hope. With a slap of his palm against the wooden desk, he turned toward the door. "We'll know tomorrow."

The suddenness of his movements took Kelly by surprise. "Should I call you when the key gets here?"

"FedEx guy hits town by nine-thirty most mornings. I'll see you then."

She listened as the door slammed shut behind him, assuring herself she'd made the right decision to believe his story. Packing, however, had lost its appeal.

She connected to the Internet using the remote number from her own account. Now was as good a time as any to study up on Oxygesic. It couldn't hurt to know exactly what she was getting herself into.

In the middle of downloading the fourth article she'd found, Frank Jones returned her call.

He confirmed Rachel had been working on an Oxygesic story, yet even more intriguing was his question regarding Rachel's notebook. *A crazy looking thing with butterflies all over it.* According to Jones, he'd never seen her without it.

Kelly leaned against the chair back after she hung up, rubbing her hands over her face then massaging her temples. Exhaustion seeped into her every muscle.

Rachel had loved to make lists and notes. Always

had. So where would she leave a notebook? Kelly searched the house from top to bottom. Between sofa cushions. Under mattresses. Behind chairs. In drawers. In closets. Finally, she retreated to the porch empty-handed, dropping into a rocker.

A gull flew past and landed on the roof of her car. *Of course.* Kelly raced into the house and dialed Information. She should have thought of this before. The notebook had probably been left in Rachel's car.

"Sheriff's office," a clipped female voice answered.

Less than a minute later, Kelly winced at the buzz of the dial tone in her ear. Apparently small towns not only took care of their own, they also didn't talk to outsiders. The woman had dismissed her by simply explaining Rachel's effects had been forwarded to her family.

Kelly dialed the phone once more. Rachel's brother answered on the third ring.

"Jim, it's Kelly."

"Kelly." He sounded exhausted and she hoped she hadn't called at a bad time—as if there could be a good time when you'd just lost your sister. "Is everything okay?" he asked. "How's the packing going?"

"I'm off to a slow start." She took her time, wanting to choose her words carefully. "I needed to ask you something."

"The rent's paid through to the end of the month," he interrupted. "So don't worry about taking your time."

Kelly squeezed her eyes shut and continued, "Jim, I'm not calling about the house. I spoke with the police and I understand the coroner has given his final determination."

"She drowned." His friendly tone evaporated, growing strained.

"There's more, isn't there?"

Silence.

"Jim?"

"The toxicology report showed drugs in her system, Kelly. It's been a great shock."

Kelly sat stunned for a moment. "She never used drugs," she said, realizing she sounded just like Dan talking about his sister.

"I don't think the results would lie." A tired sigh whispered across the line. "The family would like to keep this quiet."

"Understood." Alarm bells screamed inside Kelly's head. "Did you know she was doing a story about the very thing?"

"What do you mean?"

"Rachel was investigating an illegal drug ring. That's the reason I called. Did the police forward a notebook to you?"

"A notebook?"

"Covered with butterflies."

"No. Look, Kelly, my sister's dead. That's all I can deal with right now."

She'd pushed too hard. "Forgive me."

"No problem. I've got to go."

"Jim?" She took a deep breath, gathering her courage for one last question. "May I ask what kind of drug showed up in her system?"

"An opiate."

Kelly's mouth went dry. *A time-released opiate.* Dan's explanation bounced around her brain. "Could they tell the specific type?"

"We didn't request additional tests. What difference would it make?"

"I understand. I'm sorry, I—"

"The police did say one more thing." His words cut her short.

"Yes?" She straightened, holding her breath.

"They thought it might be something called Oxygesic. Apparently it's real popular up in those parts."

Chapter Three

Early the next morning, Kelly leaned her full weight against the smooth shower tiles, letting the steaming water pelt the small of her back. She rolled her head from the left to the right then back again to ease the knot of tension in her shoulders.

Oxygesic. She'd never heard the word before yesterday and now it was all she thought of. That and Dan Steele's breathtaking blue eyes. Those two things had haunted her dreams, the little that she'd slept.

She'd spent several restless hours realizing she might have been too quick to believe Dan's story. After all, he was a complete stranger, even if he'd been a friend of Rachel's. Yes, he'd piqued her curiosity where Rachel's death was concerned, but from now on, she'd be more cautious in following his lead.

Kelly straightened, letting the water run over the top of her head. The man might have a sound reason for wondering how Rachel and his sister had died, but Kelly didn't know him well enough to trust him, and she didn't plan to.

She'd once trusted her ex-fiancé, Brian, with all of her heart. What a lesson that had been.

Brian had entered her life like a knight in shining armor. Her parents had died in a small plane crash during one of their European jaunts. Kelly and Brian had been colleagues at a large Philadelphia advertising agency, and his kind, concerned manner had been most welcome in her time of emotional need. Hell, she'd clung to him like a love-starved puppy. He and Rachel had become all she had.

Two years later, she'd learned every move he'd made had been carefully choreographed to achieve his goal of a vice president's slot. In the end, he'd broken Kelly's heart, cost her a career and reputation, and taught her trust was an attribute highly overrated.

Kelly had been falsely accused of trading corporate secrets, and Brian had been hailed for his role in exposing her. Rachel had exploited the story for a front-page byline.

A knock sounded out front just as Kelly finished drying off her hair. She shook off the old hurt, anchored a towel around herself and rushed to open the door. An express envelope sat wedged against the screen.

Pushing the door closed behind her, she dropped onto the sofa to open the envelope. The key sat taped and folded inside a note from Jane. *Happy hunting,* was all she'd written.

A chuckle slipped from Kelly's lips, and she shook her head. Hunting was right, but she wasn't so sure how happy she and Dan would be when they found their answers.

DAN STOOD on the deck, staring at the angry morning ocean. Storm coming, he thought. His mind wandered to Rachel and Diane. *Did* they have anything in common other than the way they died?

Guilt welled from deep inside him. Maybe if he'd been more available to his sister he could have prevented her death. All he could do now was continue his search for the truth about how she'd really died.

As for Rachel, had his quest for the truth pushed her into harm's way? His gut said yes—most definitely yes—but one thing was for certain, she'd grabbed on to the story like a pit bull, as determined as he had been to find answers.

Rachel's desirability had stemmed from the fact she was a reporter. Once Dan had discovered that, he'd manipulated her investigative nature to draw her interest to Oxygesic. They'd briefly shared a physical relationship, but neither had had any interest in taking things further.

Kelly's image flashed through his mind. So much like Rachel and yet, so not like Rachel. The pull of attraction tugged at him, but he fought it. He'd slipped last night when he'd felt concern for her. As intriguing as he found the woman, he needed her for her ties to Rachel, nothing more. She was his one possibility to make a breakthrough on this investigation—his one hope at finding something that would convince Jake to go after Miller.

He glanced at his watch. Nine-fifteen. Time to find out what treasures her post-office key held.

DAN PULLED THE CAR into the gravel lot of the post office. Stones flew as he brought the car to an abrupt stop.

"Her brother said it was some kind of opiate." Kelly sat in the passenger seat, scrutinizing the key in her palm.

Dan glanced at the small, brass object, wondering what answers would be unlocked by the tiny sliver of metal. "Oxygesic?"

Kelly nodded. "He didn't know that for sure. The family didn't request more specific testing."

He gripped the steering wheel, struggling to control the frustration and anger he'd fought to keep in check ever since he'd learned of Rachel's death. "And that doesn't seem a bit convenient to you?"

"Convenient?" Kelly met his glare, curiosity shimmering in her brown gaze.

Sudden heat licked low and heavy in Dan's belly. He shoved the unwanted sensation away, retraining his focus on the mystery he so desperately needed to solve. "That she died with the very drug in her system she'd been investigating." He cut the ignition, reaching for the door.

"What if it's a coincidence?"

The uncertainty in Kelly's voice stopped him cold. He needed her with him on this if they were to find the proof he needed. "You don't believe me?"

Their gazes locked. Kelly held her ground, but didn't answer.

He pushed again. "What does your gut tell you?"

Kelly shifted in her seat. "My gut says something's up." She spoke the words softly, yet surely.

"Exactly." Dan opened the driver's door and nodded to the key now clasped in her fist. "Let's go."

"WHAT'S THE NUMBER on the key?" Dan approached the first row of post-office boxes.

"Four-three-six." Kelly ran her fingers over the metal squares. Two-twenty… Two-sixty-seven. She tipped her head. "This way."

Dan followed her into a dark corner of the post office. Sand grit beneath her sneakers, and she slipped as they rounded the last row of boxes.

"Help you folks?" A middle-aged woman leaned over the service counter.

Dan stole a quick glance in her direction. "No thanks. We're good." He leaned close to Kelly, dropping his voice to a whisper. "She must be new. I've never seen her before."

His breath brushed against Kelly's cheek, and a whisper of awareness danced down her spine. She stood still for a moment, shocked by the effect of his nearness on her senses.

He turned away, resuming his scan of the box numbers. "Found it."

His gruff tone snapped her back to reality. She stepped to where he waited and handed him the key. Dan slipped the tiny object into the lock and turned it. The mechanism clicked, and their gazes met.

Kelly's heart lurched in her throat. The now familiar determination fired from the depths of Dan's eyes. It was a determination she couldn't help but admire, even though the look rang chillingly familiar to her memories of Brian.

Dan swung the small metal door open then reached for the stack of waiting envelopes. Kelly held her breath, not knowing what she expected him to find. It wasn't as if the killer would have mailed Rachel a signed confession—would he? A small spiral notebook appeared as Dan lifted the pile. Butterfly stickers covered the red cover.

"Jackpot." Kelly reached past him to pluck the notebook from the box, gripping it tightly in her shaking hand.

"Let's get out of here." He snapped the box closed, grabbed her elbow and steered her abruptly toward the door.

The strength of his grip startled her, and she eased her arm free from his grasp. "Don't you want to—"

"Outside."

A few moments later, they sat in Dan's car, staring at the box's contents on their laps.

"What's in the envelopes?" Kelly's heart pounded. To think, just yesterday she'd thought her trip would involve nothing more than packing up Rachel's life. Now she found herself growing obsessed with discovering exactly how that life had ended—and why. She might never have the chance to make amends with Rachel, but she could make amends with her memory.

"Looks like a bunch of junk. An electric bill, a book club ad, a postcard from the chamber of commerce. What's this?" He turned an envelope in his hand. "State board of pharmacy?"

He ripped the end off the envelope and pulled out a note handwritten on professionally printed letterhead.

"Unable to reach you by phone," Dan read out loud. "Didn't want to leave a message. Call me. Think I found what you needed. 'S.'"

Excitement and hope rushed through Kelly.

Dan scowled. "'S.' How the hell am I going to find out who 'S' is?"

"What's the chamber thing?" Kelly tapped the postcard, hoping for another clue.

Dan turned over the small piece. "Business After Hours." He grimaced, meeting Kelly's gaze. "It's a business card exchange. Time of your life." He shook his head and started to rip the card in two.

Kelly snatched it from his fingers. "Maybe I should go."

His puzzled gaze captured hers and held. She steeled herself, refusing to be intimidated by his intensity. He narrowed his eyes without saying a word.

She spoke first. "Couldn't hurt to meet some people. Don't most of the local business owners attend?"

He nodded, still silent.

Kelly lifted one shoulder then let it drop. "What about the local pharmacist?"

"Don't even think it." Dan started the ignition then eased the car out of the space.

Annoyance flashed through her. "I need to know what really happened to Rachel."

"That makes two of us."

A muscle worked in his jaw as Kelly scrutinized his sharp profile. "Do you expect me to sit back and let you call the shots?"

"Wouldn't be a bad idea." Dan cast a sideways glance, one dark brow arching. "Or do you think he'll take one look at you and explain the accounting method he uses for his illegal drug sales?"

Kelly crossed her arms over her chest, her annoyance morphing into anger. "What makes you any more qualified for this than me?"

His features softened momentarily, but he seemed to catch himself, restoring his carefully controlled expression. "I know the locals."

Kelly pulled herself as tall as she could against the passenger seat. "From what I understand you spent most of your adult life up North. Didn't you just come back recently?"

A smile played against his lips for a split second. "You checked me out?"

"I said I would."

He turned to meet her gaze as if studying her face.

Kelly started at the heat sparking between them. "Just what is it you did up North?"

"Corporate development." Dan spoke the words flatly, as if he hadn't appreciated her asking.

"And now?"

He inhaled sharply. "And now I figure out what really happened to my sister…and Rachel."

They rode in silence for several long seconds. Kelly turned to stare out the side window, her focus landing on a small cemetery tucked away along the side of the road.

"Diane would have celebrated her birthday later this week." Dan's voice broke the silence. "Instead she's in there."

Kelly's heart squeezed. She turned, intending to reach for his hand, but catching herself before she made the far-too-intimate gesture. "I'm sorry."

The fact she'd come so close to touching him shocked her. She hadn't felt compelled to reach for any man since Brian had stomped all over her faith in the opposite sex, yet the raw emotion strangled inside Dan's voice had registered deep inside her. She'd have to watch herself, and her reactions.

Silence beat between them yet again.

"I'm a graphic designer," Kelly blurted out, suddenly uncomfortable with the tension squeezing the air out of the small car. "You don't suppose a business owner like a pharmacist could use a new brochure every now and then to boost business, do you?"

She turned toward Dan in time to see the lines of his profile sharpen. "Might be worth a shot." He jerked a thumb toward the colorful notebook still sitting on her lap. "Anything?"

Kelly flipped through the blank pages. "Not much. Just one word on the last page." She fanned the sheets. "And it looks like several pages are missing."

"What's the word?"

"Shakespeare."

"Shakespeare?" He grimaced, shooting a glance at Kelly. "Was she a big fan?"

"No." Kelly shook her head. "She couldn't stand him."

She stared at the word then flipped the notebook closed. Disappointment eased through her. She'd hoped the notebook would hold more than one word. At least they had the pharmacy board lead.

"Do you think 'S' could be Shakespeare?" she asked.

"I'll call and find out." Dan pulled into the drive-way of Rachel's house and cut the engine. "I'll meet you at the chamber at six. Miller shouldn't see us together."

Kelly gathered the mail and the notebook and hesitated as she climbed out of the small car. Tension still filled the space between them, but the fact he'd accepted her idea had shifted something intangible between them. "Thanks."

He nodded, averting his gaze from her face. "I'll see what I can find out about our friend Shakespeare."

She climbed to the top of the steps, pausing to watch as his car pulled away. What had Rachel gotten herself into? Whatever it was, Kelly had a sinking feeling it had gotten her killed.

DAN SAT staring through the car windshield at the Sunset Assisted Living complex. Lilac mums lined the sidewalk and hunter-green shutters framed spotless windows. The sun reflected off the bright white vinyl siding.

The building looked so calm on the outside. Orderly and neat. Nothing like the inside where minds and bodies failed—some slowly, some quickly.

His mother had been a resident for almost a year, since her dementia had worsened to the point where she needed round-the-clock care. She seemed content here, though. As content as could be expected.

Dan sat for a moment, letting his thoughts trace back over his conversation with Kelly. He shouldn't have mentioned Diane's birthday when they passed the cemetery. He wasn't a fan of sharing personal details, let alone details that hinted at weakness. Kelly and her questions had somehow burrowed beneath his skin like an itch he had no intention of scratching. He'd have to be more careful when he saw her again tonight.

Dan's stomach tightened at the thought, but he shook it off, refocusing on the building waiting before him. He pulled the key from the ignition and climbed from the small car, slamming the door shut before heading for the entrance.

"How are you doing, Dolores?"

The strawberry-blonde sitting at the reception desk looked up, flashing a warm smile as Dan pushed through the glass doors. "Pretty good, Mr. Steele. How 'bout you?"

"Can't complain." *Liar.* "Is she down in activities?"

The young woman glanced at the clock on the wall. "Should be."

"Thanks."

A long walk later, he found his mother sitting in a wingback chair facing a window. The familiar ache pulled at his heart. She deserved so much more.

The rest of the unit residents sat in a circle, tossing a beach ball from one to another. Strains of Glenn Miller filled the air.

His mother's back served as a wall between herself and the others, so unlike the vital, social woman she'd once been before her world had fallen apart.

Dan nodded to the activities aide and pulled up a chair. He put his hand on the arm of his mother's chair, letting his gaze follow hers.

Gulls floated in the breeze above the sound. Sunshine glistened off the surface of the water, broken only by the wake of a small sailboat headed back toward the marina.

"Mom."

She turned to face him, her soft white hair seeming to have grown even thinner since last week, her pale blue eyes more milky.

"It's me, Dan."

"I know who you are." She turned her attention back to the window. "How's your sister?"

"She's d… She's okay, Mom." He'd probably go to hell for lying to her, but why not?

"I saw him kill her, you know."

His pulse quickened. "What?"

His mother's gaze stayed fixed on the sound. She raised her hand, pointing a bony finger toward the water. "Right there. I tried to tell her. They wouldn't let me tell her."

She lowered her hand to her lap and fingered the zipper on her housecoat.

"Who, Mom? Diane?"

"No." She frowned, the grimace accentuating the wrinkles left by age and the life she'd loved alongside the ocean. "The other girl. I tried to tell her, but they wouldn't let me."

"I don't understand, Mom. Who?"

"At the market. I saw her at the market." She looked at him with searching eyes, gripping his hand with a force that shocked him. "She's dead, Danny. I saw him kill her and they wouldn't let me tell her." She looked back toward the water. "They made me leave."

Sadness squeezed Dan's heart, twisted his stomach. His mother had never done a thing to deserve this fate—this smothering disease that nibbled away at her mind a little more with each passing day.

"Wouldn't let me tell her." Her voice trailed off into a faint whisper.

Not fair at all, Dan thought.

KELLY PULLED into the lot outside the chamber's office a little before six. The warm architecture made the building look more like a home than a professional building. People milled about on the covered porch, shaking hands, patting backs and sipping drinks.

She climbed out of her Jetta and checked her purse one last time. She tucked her business-card holder into the back pocket of the bag, making it easily accessible. Head high, Kelly took a deep breath, smoothing her skirt before heading for the entrance.

A middle-aged woman with short gray hair greeted her at the top of the steps. "I'm Barb Parker," she said with an outstretched hand. "Welcome to the chamber. Are you a guest this evening?"

"I am." Kelly shook the woman's hand, giving her warmest smile. "I spoke to you earlier today on the phone. I'm Kelly Weir."

"Well, welcome." The woman's demeanor slipped from pleasant to curious in the span of a split second. "So sorry about your friend, Rachel. Have you finished packing up her house?"

"Working on it."

"Come on in. Let's get you a name tag and get you introduced around." She put her hand on the back of Kelly's shoulder, steering her toward the registration table. "What was it you do again?"

"Public Relations and Marketing." Kelly concentrated on tamping down the nerves clawing their way up her throat. "Graphic design… Writing."

The next few minutes passed in a whirlwind of handshakes, greetings and smiles. Kelly wondered if she would ever remember any of these names.

"Ms. Weir." A gruff voice behind her made her jump. Kelly spun around. "How are you getting settled in?" Frank Healey, the Realtor who'd given her the key to Rachel's house stood smiling, his expression expectant.

"Fine, thanks," Kelly said, relieved to see a familiar face. "It's good to see you."

"You, too. This is my wife, Marge."

Kelly shook hands with a plump woman of about fifty. Her blond hair fell smartly in a short crop. She wore no makeup, and her skin showed the wrinkles that came from years of sun exposure.

"It's nice to meet you." Marge nodded thoughtfully, measuring Kelly. "Frank said you looked like Rachel. He was right."

"I've heard that most of my life." Kelly smiled. "I take it as a compliment."

"You should." The skin around Marge's eyes softened. "Rachel was a lovely girl. Such a shame."

"Horrible accident." A deep ache blossomed in Kelly's chest. She straightened, feeling a renewed determination to get to the bottom of what had actually happened.

"Well." Marge looked over both shoulders and leaned toward Kelly, dropping her voice to a whisper. "I heard it was drugs."

Kelly pasted on a shocked expression. As much as she hated gossips, she might have hit the jackpot with Marge Healey.

"Margie," Frank snapped.

Marge shrugged. "I was shocked to hear it. Not that I'd ever speak ill of the dead."

Frank cleared his throat, his expression amused. "You need to know anything in this town, Margie's your gal. Dead or not, she's got the latest dirt on everyone."

Sadness flickered through Kelly. Had Rachel changed so much these people wouldn't question drugs in her system? It didn't seem possible. "I don't believe she'd use drugs." She directed the comment to Marge, hoping for an explanation.

Marge pressed her lips together, shooting a glance at Frank.

"The thought is she got hooked while she worked at the institute," he said.

"The institute?" Kelly frowned.

"Serenity Pain Institute." Marge gave a shake of her short hair. "She didn't last long. Last I heard she was a freelance reporter."

"We called that out of a job in my day." Frank fell silent as his gaze landed on Kelly's serious stance.

"Are you enjoying it here?" He patted Kelly's arm, obviously trying to change the subject. "As much as you can under the circumstances."

"I am. But, I can't help admitting I'm concerned about Rachel's death. Do you think one of her stories got her into trouble?"

Frank and Marge exchanged a quick glance. Kelly's pulse quickened. She'd obviously struck a chord.

"Now why would you ask that?" Marge gave a tight smile. "Someone been putting ideas in your head?" Marge touched her fingertips to Kelly's shoulder. "Don't go looking for trouble where there is none."

The woman's comment didn't sit well. Kelly's instincts screamed that trouble was exactly what Rachel had discovered, and as the result of her work.

"You folks are monopolizing this young lady's time." A deep voice rumbled from behind her, pricking the hairs on the back of her neck to attention.

She turned, chilled instantly by the coldest pair of blue eyes she'd ever seen.

"Vince Miller." The man extended a hand. "Pleased to meet you."

Chapter Four

The woman on the other end of the phone let out an exasperated sigh.

"I know it's a tall order," Dan said. "But I need a list of your employees whose first names start with 'S'. Someone left me a message and I couldn't make out what they said. It's urgent I reach whoever it was." He mentally crossed his fingers. If the woman bought his version of the truth, she just might help.

"You do know it's after hours and I'm the last one here," she replied. "I was just locking up. Why don't you call back tomorrow?"

Dan glanced at his watch. Five forty-five. He had to get going to meet Kelly at the chamber. The last thing he wanted was for her to be alone with Miller without him close by.

"I apologize, and I appreciate your time. I do." He thought for a moment then asked, "What about Shakespeare? Anyone named Shakespeare?"

"Is this a crank call?" The woman's tone grew incredulous. "Are you doing this on a dare?"

"I'm quite serious. As I mentioned, the message was garbled."

"There's no one by that name."

"What about other names with an 'S'?"

She rattled through a list of several names, apparently choosing to answer Dan's request in an effort to end the call. He asked for the extensions of two—Susan in Regulatory and Scott in Inspections.

After leaving a brief voice mail message for each, he dashed out the door for the chamber meeting. Hopefully Miller wouldn't zero in on Kelly until he got there.

VINCE MILLER stood at least six foot four. His jet-black hair hung in waves, tapering behind his ears to frame his slender face. His piercing stare sent a deep chill through Kelly.

"I understand you're clearing out Rachel's things." Miller smiled and leaned close.

She took an instinctive step backward, doing her best to focus on her goal and not the subtle trembling of her nerves. "Yes. It's going slowly. I'm thinking about staying for a bit, actually."

"Barb Parker tells me you do some design work." His icy gaze widened expectantly.

"I do." Kelly nodded. "If you know of anyone who needs some help, keep me in mind. I wouldn't mind lining up some clients down here. Good business trip, you know."

Lord, she was babbling. She had to pull it together. Reaching into her purse, she slipped a business card from the case and handed it to Miller.

"Thanks." He took her offered card then pulled his own from his shirt pocket. "I run Miller's Apothecary, but I do freelance photography on the side. Would you be interested in helping me come up with something?" He looked directly into her eyes, sending a flash of dread rippling through her. "For the photography?"

"What did you have in mind?" Kelly concentrated on remaining calm, acting natural. "I'm not sure how long I'll be in town. But, I'd be happy to help you all I can."

"Maybe we could start with a brochure." He straightened, obviously pleased she'd shown an interest. "When can we meet to talk details?"

The conversation felt too easy. Kelly's insides squirmed.

"Do you have a shop?" She willed her brain to kick into design mode. She needed to appear sincerely interested in his business if the plan was going to work. "If I could see some of your shots, that would help me."

"Actually, I keep my portfolio at the pharmacy. Can you come by tomorrow? I'll treat you to lunch."

"You don't have to do that." Kelly shook her head. The less time alone with this guy, the better. "But I'll come by around 11:00 a.m. Is that okay?"

"It's a date."

His words sent a fresh whisper of apprehension dancing along her spine. She inhaled deeply, looking away for a brief moment. Dan stood at the periphery of her vision. She couldn't deny the relief that flooded through her at the sight of him. She had no plans to grow dependant on the man, as she had on Brian, but felt safe just knowing he was near.

Vince took her hand in his, shaking it once more. "It's been my great pleasure to meet you. See you tomorrow at eleven."

Kelly nodded, slipping her hand free from his grasp as soon as she could without appearing rude.

"Maybe you'll reconsider lunch," Vince added before he walked away.

Kelly found herself staring after him, her nerves raw. Lunch? She'd be afraid she'd end up on the menu instead of reading it. She wiped her palm on the side of her skirt, trying to shake off the ice-cold pinpricks persisting at the nape of her neck.

DAN WATCHED as Miller and Kelly talked, careful to stay out of their line of sight. A protectiveness welled inside him. Even though the two couldn't be in a more public place, he didn't like the look in Miller's eyes—like a mountain lion sizing up his prey.

Miller smiled, leaning toward Kelly. Dan quelled his desire to close the distance, grab the man and drag him far from where Kelly stood. Dan had always prided himself on maintaining control, but the glimpses of vulnerability he'd spotted in Kelly had started to chip away at his protective shell. He'd have to watch himself.

Based on the glint in Miller's cold eyes, involving Kelly might have been unwise. Yet the business card exchange had been her idea, and judging from the look of their conversation, Miller had bought her design idea hook, line and sinker.

Dan knew he should feel hopeful to have a fresh in with the pharmacist, but he couldn't help but feel concern. Kelly had stepped smack in the middle of Miller's radar screen, when experience told him he should have steered her clear.

She met his eye for a split second, and Dan's stomach caught. Color flushed her cheeks. Because she'd seen him? Or because of something Miller had said?

Miller released his grip on Kelly's hand and moved away. Dan flattened himself against the wall until the other man left the building, presumably heading back to his store.

He stepped to Kelly's side, and her dark gaze danced with excitement as their eyes locked.

"Well?"

"Too easy," she muttered under her breath.

He cupped her elbow, shocked again by his over-powering desire to remove her from harm's way. He led her to an empty corner of the porch. "What happened?"

"He wants me to do a brochure for his photography."

"Photography?" Dan nodded to a passing couple. "That was quick. I should have known Miller wouldn't waste any time." He slipped his hand inside her arm, guiding her toward the exit, all the while aware of the soft feel of her flesh beneath his fingers. "We need to discuss this."

Kelly moved free of his touch. "I won't let you talk me out of this."

He took a step back, measuring the flash of life

in the depths of her glare. The woman had determination, no doubt about it, but he had to make sure she didn't do something foolish. He jerked his thumb toward the parking lot. "Too many ears around here. I'll buy you dinner."

"Not necessary." She visibly bristled.

His admiration turned to impatience. "Do you want to get to the bottom of Rachel's death, or not?"

Kelly moved past him, her elbow brushing against his side. The contact disarmed him, anchoring his feet to the porch floor.

She stopped, pivoting on one heel to level a curious glance in his direction. "Something wrong?"

Silence beat between them. Dan shook his head, willing his body forward. He pressed his palm to the small of her back, amazed by the tension coiling inside him.

"Not a thing."

Only, at that particular moment, aware of her body's heat beneath the fabric of her blouse and the protective urges building inside him, he was beginning to think his control might have met its match.

KELLY'S BREATH caught as she settled into her seat inside the intimate bar and grill. Streaks of peach and melon illuminated the sky as the sun slipped beyond the sound, the water reflecting the colors in shimmering ripples.

She'd done nothing but relive her conversation with Miller as she'd followed Dan to the restaurant. She held her thoughts until the waiter had taken their drink orders, but once he'd moved away from the table, she leaned forward. "Do you find it odd Miller approached me so quickly about the brochure?"

"I thought about that on the way over, but I'd bet he wants to find out if you know what Rachel knew."

She frowned. "Why would he think I'd know anything?"

Dan shook his head. "Why not? You're living in her house. If he did kill her, don't you think he might wonder if she left any clues behind?"

Kelly measured his expression carefully. Wasn't that exactly what Dan had thought? That he'd find whatever notes Rachel had left behind? She considered their conversations to date, her desire to discover the truth about Rachel's death and his desire to discover the truth behind his sister's.

"Maybe he's using me." When she spoke the words, it wasn't Miller she referred to.

"Just promise you'll be careful."

Dan's voice stopped her cold—a mixture of concern and caring—dialing up the conflict simmering inside her. Kelly's pulse quickened, and their gazes locked. "I'm always careful."

His stare deepened. "Point taken."

During dinner Dan told Kelly of his call to the pharmacy board, and listened intently as she told him about the Healeys' warning.

"The Healeys said something that didn't sit well with me." Her stomach wound into a tight knot as she spoke the words, not wanting to lay her cards on the table regarding her friendship with Rachel, but needing to know more about the friend who'd become a stranger.

"They didn't seem surprised to think Rachel had drugs in her system," she continued. She shook her head and let out a sigh. "I'm wondering how much she'd changed since I spoke to her."

"How long had it been?" Genuine interest sounded in his tone, tossing the knot in Kelly's stomach onto its side.

"A year."

"Why so long?"

"She let me down." And Kelly had let them both down with her stubbornness, but he didn't need to know that.

"Why offer to take care of her things?"

"Her brother asked me." Kelly gave a quick shrug. "It's too late to fix things between us. I figured I could at least help out."

He reached across the table, closing his hand over top of hers. She didn't squirm, didn't flinch, instead allowed herself the comfort of the unexpected gesture.

Dan glanced at their joined hands then lifted his focus to her face, heat pouring from his gaze into hers. "Rachel hated drugs. All the more reason to believe someone killed her."

Kelly swallowed, stunned by the ferocity of his tone and the emotion swirling through his eyes. She wiggled her fingers free from beneath his, clasping her hands together in her lap, safely distanced from his touch. "Thanks."

AFTER DINNER Dan walked Kelly across the parking lot toward her car, mentally berating himself for reaching for her hand. He needed to maintain emotional distance from this woman. Even though he and Rachel had only been friends, he'd let down his guard, not anticipating the depth of the danger she'd put herself in. He wouldn't repeat the mistake with Kelly. To stay sharp he needed to stay objective.

"I'll follow you tomorrow to Miller's."

Kelly spun to face him, surprise shimmering in her dark gaze. "Surely you don't think he's a risk to me at his own store?"

A lock of auburn hair blew across her face, and he captured the strand between his fingers, tucking the silky length behind her ear.

He dropped his hand quickly to his side and shrugged. "I'd rather play things safe from here on out." He didn't want to tell her he was afraid Miller would escalate, moving quickly if he suspected Kelly was on to his illegal activities.

Her eyes searched his face, then she nodded without argument, as if sensing there was no talking him out of his decision. "Fair enough."

She turned, and they walked in silence toward their cars. At the sound of Kelly's sudden intake of breath, Dan's nerve endings snapped to attention.

Her Jetta sat close to the asphalt—too close. He stepped quickly to inspect the damage. All four tires had been slashed.

Miller.

Dan felt Kelly's warmth as she drew up close to his side. She stood wide-eyed, her hand pressed to her throat. "Who would do this?"

"Who do you think?"

Miller must have developed an immediate obsession with Kelly, or else he'd sensed her graphic design offer had been anything but innocent. Either way, there was no telling what he might do next.

Dan pulled his cell phone from his pocket. "I'll call my repair shop. They'll get out here first thing tomorrow."

"Don't you want to call the police?"

"For what? They'll write it off as a teenage prank." Dan shook his head. "It's easier to deal with the repair and keep this to ourselves. I'll drive you home."

As they drove down the long, dark stretch of road that linked Corolla to Summer Shores, Kelly's heartbeat had yet to return to a normal rate.

"If you want to back out of your meeting with Miller, you can." The rumble of Dan's voice sliced through the tense silence inside his car.

Did she want to back out? She could finish packing and go home now. She could walk away. But if she did so, would she ever be able to forgive herself for not digging into the questions swirling beneath the official explanation of Rachel's death? If she left Summer Shores now, she'd be ignoring Rachel for a second time.

"I'll go." Her tone grew sharp as she answered Dan.

She glanced at his profile in time to see him nod into the darkness.

The cemetery appeared alongside the car as they neared Summer Shores' city limits, and Kelly's heart ached for the sister Dan had lost.

"How old would Diane have been?"

"Twenty-four." He spoke the words slowly, his voice dropping low. "Tomorrow."

Kelly reached for him, this time not censoring the gesture. She pressed her fingertips to his shoulder, her focus zeroing in on the way his jaw tensed as she made contact. "I'm sorry."

He nodded. She dropped her hand back into her lap. Neither spoke again until he pulled the car into the driveway outside Rachel's house.

"I'll make sure your car's here first thing."

Kelly reached for the door. "Thanks."

"Lock up tight tonight."

His parting words sent a shiver up her spine as she straightened from the car.

At the top of the steps, Kelly turned, watching the taillights fade into the night. If she wasn't mistaken, they'd both turned a corner, each revealing a bit more of their personal pain than they'd intended.

From now on, she'd have to keep her focus on uncovering the truth about Miller and any role he'd played in Rachel's death. She'd also have to watch her back. Even if it wasn't Miller, whoever had slashed the tires on her car had meant business, obviously not happy with her presence in Summer Shores.

The small hairs at the base of her neck pricked to attention, as if someone watched her from the inky depths of the foliage at her back. Kelly slid her key into the lock just as a twig snapped in the distance. Adrenaline surged through her veins.

"Who's there?" She called out into the pitch-black night, knowing in her head the noise was likely nothing more than an animal out on his evening rounds.

She stepped inside, locking the door quickly behind her, doing her best to will away the sense of dread that had settled heavily in her bones.

THE CAMERA SHUTTER clicked again and again as he focused on the girl. She'd spent too much time with Steele tonight. He hadn't liked seeing them together. Not at all.

Now that her car was out of commission, perhaps she'd stay where she needed to be—inside the house, packing up Rachel's belongings.

When a crack of light spilled onto the deck from the bedroom door, he ducked low behind the bushes.

She stepped outside, coming to a stop at the railing. He longed to capture her on film, her beautiful, upturned face luminous in the pale glow of the moon. Her nightshirt exposed long, lean legs and her dark hair shimmered in the ethereal light.

He couldn't risk the noise of pressing the shutter. He'd have to immortalize the shot in his mind.

She turned and disappeared into the bedroom, closing the door behind her. If only she'd open the blinds.

He'd like to watch her sleep.

Chapter Five

Kelly pulled Vince Miller's business card out of her leather portfolio and double-checked the address. Milepost 11 off of Highway 12. She glanced to her right. Milepost 10. Getting close. She slowed, grateful Dan's repair shop had been so quick to replace her tires and deliver her car.

She spotted the Miller's Apothecary sign and braked to avoid missing the driveway. She glanced in her rearview mirror, relief flooding through her as Dan's car pulled to the side of the road partway down the block. He'd told her she had twenty minutes before he'd make an appearance, and he'd given her strict instructions to run at the first sign of trouble.

Anticipation bubbled in Kelly's veins as she stepped inside. The store itself sat small and dark. End caps full of suntan lotion and lip balm crowded the entrance. A young girl chewing gum glanced up from a magazine at the checkout counter when an electronic beep signaled Kelly had passed some sort of detector.

"Kelly," Vince's voice called out. "Back here."

She followed a narrow aisle of shampoo, conditioner and hair spray toward the back of the store. The pharmacy sat along the back wall, and Vince leaned over the counter, the area elevated at least a foot above the main floor.

"It's great to see you." His calculated gaze sent an instant chill racing through her.

"Thanks." Kelly fisted her clammy palms. Maybe this had been a lousy idea. In all probability, this man had spent last night slashing her car tires. Now he stood smiling down at her like a cat about to eat a canary.

"Why don't we go in the back? I'll show you my photography." Vince turned to a second young girl. "Sarah, this is Kelly Weir. She's going to be helping me promote my photography services."

"Nice to meet you." The young girl's raven hair swung about her ears as she nodded. "I've heard a lot about you."

What on earth did she mean? Kelly's mind raced.

"This way." Vince held open a half door, pointing to a larger door at the back of the work area.

"Nice to meet you, too," Kelly said as she brushed past the girl.

Vince led the way into a storage room more crowded than the store itself, not that Kelly had thought that possible. Boxes of inventory sat stacked in piles, the smell of cardboard battling with the scent of citrus air freshener.

"Welcome to my secret hideaway." Vince's flat tone triggered trembling deep in the pit of Kelly's stomach.

She shot him a polite smile. His sweet cologne tangled with the dank air in the small space, and her stomach clenched. She couldn't get out of here soon enough. "Did you have some samples you wanted me to look at?"

"Are you always in a rush to work?" Vince took a step toward her. "I'd love to have the time to get to know you. It's not every day I get such a lovely visitor."

Kelly stood her ground, determined to hide her apprehension. "Vince, don't take this the wrong way, but I'm looking for a strictly professional relationship."

He held his hands up in a mock gesture of defeat. "No offense taken." He cast a sideways leer in Kelly's direction before he began his search, making her wonder how seriously he'd taken her words.

A few moments later, he pulled a leather case from beneath a stack of folders. "Here they are." Loose glossy prints slipped to the floor.

Kelly knelt beside him, gathering the dropped shots. She plucked an assortment of landscapes, portraits, product shots and still lifes from the faded linoleum. All different. All beautiful. "You've got a real gift." And he did.

Her brain worked feverishly, trying to reconcile the talent and creativity displayed before her with the image Dan had painted of the man.

"Thanks." Vince's fingers brushed hers as she handed him the last print, eliciting a fresh wave of nerves.

Kelly quickly stood and took a few steps back,

making a show of jotting down a thought in her note-book. "Do you want to specialize in one area or are you trying to promote everything?"

"What do you think?"

What did she think? She thought the quicker she could talk her way out of the cramped room, the better. She pasted on her best professional smile. "I'd suggest a brochure that touches on each area. If you'd pick out some of your favorites, I'll scan them into graphics files and return your originals. They'll make a gorgeous brochure."

They talked for a few more minutes about the actual brochure design, and Kelly promised to work up a sample within the next few days.

"I hope it won't be that long before I see you again." Vince's pale eyes widened, sending a shudder down Kelly's spine.

"Of course not." She forced the words over her lips, hoping she sounded enthusiastic even though she felt anything but.

"Do you have a number where I can reach you?"

"Sure, I'm at Rachel's old house." She reached in her backpack, fumbling for a pen.

"I've got one. Over here."

He motioned to a counter cluttered with paperwork. Large bottles sat piled to one side, the lettering unmistakable. Oxygesic.

"Wow. This must be a big seller." Kelly nonchalantly tipped her head, her heartbeat drumming in her ears. She prayed he couldn't hear the pounding rhythm.

"What?" Vince picked up a bottle. "This? It's for the institute."

"The institute?"

"Serenity Pain Institute." Vince sat the bottle back on the counter. "Cancer. Chronic pain. They're the biggest around. It's great for me. I'm the only pharmacy for miles that carries this drug."

"Why? Don't your competitors want a piece of the pie?"

He patted a bottle top. "Big theft risk. Kids like to get high." He turned to her and smiled. "Their loss is my gain." He shrugged. "I don't worry about the theft. No one would dare mess with me."

Vince rubbed his thumb and forefinger together, smirking. "The institute is very good for my bottom line. Know what I mean?"

DAN LET OUT a relieved breath as Kelly dashed across the parking lot to her car. He lowered his window as her Jetta approached then slowed to a stop.

Her slender face was flushed, her brown eyes even brighter than usual. Like a deer caught in the headlights, actually.

"You okay?" The husky quality of his voice gave away exactly how concerned he'd been.

Kelly's gaze widened. "I'm fine, but he's up to something."

Excitement pulsed through Dan. "What happened?"

Kelly lowered her voice, leaning slightly out of her window. The sun caught her hair, illuminating countless shimmers of red in the long, satin strands.

"I'm not a pharmacist—" she squinted "—but his back room is packed full of Oxygesic. Says it's all for the institute."

"That can't be right." Dan cranked the ignition. The Karmann Ghia's motor purred to life. "I'll stop by in a bit. I want to pay a call on a buddy of mine at the sheriff's department."

Kelly nodded then pulled away.

A short while later Dan wished he'd skipped the visit to his old friend.

Jake had launched into a full-blown lecture. "There are three points you failed to learn when you read *Police Work for Dummies* or whatever it was that made you feel qualified to dig into this imaginary conspiracy."

Dan leveled a glare at Jake, hoping the look would stop his friend cold. No such luck.

"Motive. Means. Opportunity." Jake ticked off the points on his fingers. "Do you honestly think I haven't thought this all through?"

"I heard about the coroner's report." Dan straightened, not willing to cave under the weight of Jake's condescending tone.

"Heard what?" Jake twirled a pencil in one hand and tapped his free fingers against the cluttered top of his desk.

"An opiate was found in Rachel's system. You know it's Oxygesic. Why didn't you tell me?"

"Maybe because it's none of your business and I didn't want you to have anything else to get all worked up over."

"None of my business? She was my friend." Dan slapped his palm against Jake's desk then unfurled himself from the chair, pacing the length of the cramped office. "How many people have to die before you do something? It's all coming from Miller."

"Whoa, whoa, whoa." Jake ran a hand over his face. "You're jumping to conclusions. Yes, she had drugs in her system. Guess what? People love the stuff." He grimaced. "This is exactly why I didn't tell you."

"She was in the middle of investigating a story on the same drug." Dan leaned on Jake's desk. "You don't think that's significant?"

"No." Jake sat back, his complacent expression sending a wave of annoyance through Dan.

"What if she was too close to the truth and somebody took her out?" Dan worked to keep his simmering anger under control.

"Oh, that's good." Jake laughed without emotion. "You think someone shoved a pill down her throat and threw her in the ocean?"

Dan raised a brow.

"For the love of Pete." Jake's voice tightened as if the entire conversation caused him pain. "Do you have any idea how popular this stuff is getting? Maybe she decided to try it out, lost her head and took a swim."

"With her clothes on?" Dan concentrated on keeping his anger in check. He prided himself on maintaining his cool, and he wasn't about to lose it in front of Jake.

"Drugs, Danny." Jake shook his head. "People do crazy things."

Jake's reasoning ratcheted up Dan's anger, now knotted in his chest. He spun on his heel, turning to leave, but pausing at the door. "When this is over, I'll prove you wrong."

"I'm not wrong." Jake stood, crossing his arms over his chest. "I never am."

KELLY CROSSED the post office parking lot and pressed the button on her key fob to open the car door. There had been nothing new in the box. What did she expect? It had been little more than twenty-four hours since she and Dan had first checked Rachel's mail.

The chill of Miller's back room clung to her like a damp shawl. The guy definitely set off every internal alarm she had. No wonder Dan believed he was to blame for the Oxygesic problem. But was Miller capable of murder?

She pictured the ice-blue of his eyes and shivered. She wasn't sure she wanted to find out.

"Why did you come back?" A woman's gentle voice rattled Kelly from her thoughts.

She focused on the source, looking directly into the face of the old woman from the grocery store. Kelly stepped back with a start.

"Who do you think I am?" She leaned toward the small figure. "Do you think I'm Rachel?"

"I'm not crazy." The woman spoke in a low, quiet voice. "I saw him kill you." She tapped her index finger to her own cheekbone. "With my own eyes."

"Maddie." A male voice rang out through the crisp, fall air. A young man raced across the post office parking lot toward the woman who had started to cry.

"Don't let him hurt you again." Tears slid down her weathered cheeks. "You have to believe me."

Kelly stared, dazed, at the man, her mind swirling with confusion and questions. "She must think she knows me. I'm sorry I've upset her like this."

"Don't worry about it." He paused and looked at Kelly. "She wanders away a lot and gets confused."

Kelly reached out to touch the woman's sleeve then awkwardly pulled back. "I'm sorry."

The young man took hold of the woman's elbow, gently leading her away.

"Why won't you let me tell her?" The woman's pained tone caused Kelly's heart to ache. "I need to tell her. Why won't you let me?"

Kelly leaned against her car, goose bumps spreading over her arms. What on earth had she gotten herself into?

HE MOVED QUICKLY through her house. Who knew when she'd be back? He'd felt compelled to be inside her space—like a spider checking his web. After all, he'd been in the neighborhood and her driveway had been empty.

He opened the closet, wanting to touch her clothes. The colors and fabrics assaulted him visually and he snarled, recognizing them as Rachel's.

He looked around the room, spotting a duffel bag propped on top of a chair. He yanked open the nylon fabric to expose her clothes, neatly folded inside.

So she was living out of a duffel bag. That was promising, maybe she didn't plan to dig too deeply into Rachel's death after all.

He flipped back the comforter and lifted a pillow to his face, inhaling deeply. Fresh. Clean. He tossed the pillow back to the bed and strolled to the French doors.

Just as he pulled them open, a ball of gray fur flew at him, yowling. A cat. He hated cats. Nothing more than overgrown rodents with long tails.

He swung a foot, but missed. The furry attacker raced down the hall, stopping partway to hiss, standing and arching its back.

"Who do you think you are? Her protector?" He held one foot high above the floor. "Don't tempt me."

The cat's back rippled as it yowled again. He held his hands over his ears and stepped onto the deck. Now was as good a time as any to make his exit. The cat had given him the creeps.

He trotted down the back steps and slipped into the foliage. The cat's appearance had been fortuitous, actually. She'd think the fur ball had pushed open the doors. He laughed and shook his head.

Some things were so easy he just knew they were meant to be.

THE PHONE was ringing as Dan opened his front door. Anger still coursed through him from his conversation with Jake. He'd stopped home before going to Kelly's in the hope of calming himself. He had no intention of letting her see him this out of control.

He snatched the receiver from its base. "Yes."

"I was trying to reach Dan Steele," a male voice spoke tentatively.

"Speaking."

"You left a message for me. My name is Scott Jansen."

Dan's pulse quickened. "At the pharmacy board?"

"Yes."

He slid into a chair, pressing a palm to his forehead. He had to think clearly. Now was not the time to say something to scare this guy off.

"Thanks for calling back. I'm a friend of Rachel Braxton's." He paused for a moment, hoping to take the right approach. "I wonder if you might have been helping with some of her research?"

"It's not something I care to discuss over the phone," Jansen replied. "And I have no idea who you are."

Dan spoke cautiously. "I can understand that. Perhaps I can meet you somewhere—"

Jansen cut him off. "What I'd really like is to get in touch with Rachel. I have something for her."

"You don't know?" Cold realization seeped through Dan. Jansen had no idea she was dead.

"Know what?"

"Rachel's dead. I believe—"

The line clicked dead. Dan stared at the receiver in his hand. Scott Jansen. "S."

He pulled the pharmacy board number from his wallet and dialed. Jansen didn't pick up his extension, and Dan didn't leave a message.

I have something for her. Jansen's words echoed in Dan's mind. He might have scared the guy off, but he knew where to find him. And he would.

KELLY UNLOCKED the front door and stepped into the living room. She dropped the folders and photos from Miller on the kitchen table and set the coffeemaker to brew. Between Miller and seeing the old woman again, she was freezing, unable to shake the chill that had settled in her bones.

She padded down the hall toward the bedroom and stopped short. The French doors to the deck sat wide open. Her heart slammed against her chest. Had someone gotten in? Was whoever had slashed her tires in the house with her now? Miller?

She backed quickly toward the front door, but stumbled over something soft. Edgar looked up at her and mewed, gold eyes wide.

"Sorry, buddy." She scooped him into her arms. "You're going to be the death of me." Her words came in a rush of relieved breath as she realized he must be her intruder. "I've got to double-check every door with you around, don't I?"

The cat yowled.

"What's the matter? You don't want to be held?"

Edgar rubbed his head against her chin and began to purr.

"That's better. Perfect timing, too. I needed a good hug."

She stepped into the bedroom, shut the doors and locked them. She turned to deposit Edgar onto the bed, but stopped short. The comforter and pillow sat in total disarray.

She laughed, giving the top of Edgar's head a quick rub before she set him down. "Glad you made yourself at home while you waited." She threw the comforter over the pillow then pulled off her heels.

"Let's get some comfy clothes on, warm up and then we'll go in search of your momma. Deal?"

The cat rubbed against her. Back and forth. Mewing and purring. He leaped from the bed to the floor and sat in front of the French doors, staring into the dense foliage behind the house.

If Kelly didn't know better, she'd swear he fancied himself on guard duty.

Kelly had just taken her first sip of coffee when she heard footsteps on the steps.

Helen knocked on the door as she pushed it open. "Woo-hoo. Kelly?"

Kelly warmed at the sight of the neighbor, happy to see a friendly face. "Coffee?"

Helen shook her head and tipped it toward Edgar. "How'd the little devil do it this time?"

"French doors."

Helen frowned. "That's odd. He never liked those back steps. The burrs in the weeds hurt his feet." She tapped her fingers against her palm.

Kelly shrugged and pulled out a chair from the table. "I guess there's a first for everything."

"Hope he didn't scare you."

Kelly shook her head. "Not too badly. And he made himself at home while he waited. Even pulled back the comforter on the bed."

A crease formed between Helen's eyebrows as she sank onto a chair. "He knows better than that."

Kelly patted the woman's hand and laughed. "I don't mind." She sat down opposite Helen and slid the pile of folders from Miller to the side.

"What's that?" Helen's expression brightened.

"I'm designing a brochure for Vince Miller." The familiar dread clawed its way up from Kelly's gut. She tamped it down, doing her best to focus on Helen's visit and not on the chill that still persisted.

Helen visibly shuddered then shook her head, leveling a glare at Kelly. "He's bad news."

Kelly leaned forward expectantly. "What do you mean?"

"He doesn't deal well when women don't return his affections." She nodded. "You're just his type." The older woman's features wrinkled. "What are you doing working for him? Thought you weren't staying long."

Kelly shrugged. "I'm not, but he asked and I figured what the heck." She felt guilty lying, but it was probably for the best to keep her investigative partnership with Dan quiet.

Helen pursed her lips, nodding toward the folders. "This his stuff?"

Kelly slid the photos from the stack. "Apparently he dabbles in photography."

"Stalker," Helen mumbled.

Shocked, Kelly stared at Helen. "Is there something you should be telling me? Something specific?"

"Your friend Rachel wasn't a fan of his, that's all." Helen continued to study the photos without looking up.

"Well—" Kelly's voice dropped to a murmur "—she was investigating him, so that might be why."

"More like fending him off." Helen pressed her lips into a tight line then lifted her gaze to Kelly's.

"She couldn't get rid of the guy." She nodded toward the photos. "Then he left her a picture of herself. Really scared her."

Kelly wrapped her arms around her waist. "Of herself?"

Helen nodded, pulling the photos closer to flip through them. She stopped at a close-up of a lovely young woman and whistled.

"What?" Kelly asked.

"This is Rachel's friend."

"Who?"

"Yvonne something." Helen looked up, frowning at Kelly's questioning stare. "She died about a year ago. Car accident." She looked back at the photo. "I didn't know Miller was stalking her, too."

"Stalking is a harsh term, don't you think?"

"Not if it's accurate."

Kelly took a sip of her coffee and let the hot liquid warm her throat. A connection clicked in her mind, and excitement buzzed through her. "Rachel had a friend who died here. She thought because of drugs." She tapped the photo. "Could this be the same friend?"

Helen shrugged, shaking her head. "Could be. Just know she's dead, too." She stood and patted Kelly's hand. "Be careful. Promise me that."

"I promise," Kelly said.

She sat quietly for a long while after Helen and Edgar left. She wasn't sure how much time had passed when gravel crunched in the driveway. Footsteps pounded up the steps seconds later. When Dan cleared the threshold, he stopped, scanning the photos spread across the length of the table.

Kelly mentally scolded herself as warmth un-furled deep inside her at the sight of him. Surely the response was due to the excitement of their quest, nothing more. She shifted her concentration from Dan to Miller's photographs.

"Helen just told me Vince was stalking Rachel." She tapped the photo of Yvonne, doing her best to focus on the conversation and not on the scent of spiced soap clinging to Dan. "And this person."

He leaned close, scrutinizing the photo. "Yvonne Smithers." He shook his head. "What a waste."

He raised his gaze to meet Kelly's and she shot him a questioning look.

"She got messed up one night and drove her car into a pole."

"Helen said she was Rachel's friend."

He nodded. "Rachel was devastated." His expres-sion intensified. "This is the friend I told you about. The reason Rachel went after the story."

He stepped back, watching Kelly so closely her pulse quickened. She reminded herself any interest reflected in his stare was the result of the case, noth-ing more. Like Brian, Dan viewed her as a means to an end. Her heart couldn't afford to forget that fact.

"Rachel blamed Oxygesic for Yvonne's death," he continued. "Yvonne got hooked. Rachel always felt she'd still be alive if the drug weren't so prevalent around here."

Kelly pulled her knees up under her chin, feeling compelled to tell him about the rest of her day. "I stopped by the post office on my way home to check the box, and I ran into the same woman from the grocery store."

"What woman?"

Confusion surged through her. "I didn't tell you?"

"Apparently not." Curiosity flickered across his face.

"When I was shopping the other day, a woman told me I was dead. That she saw someone kill me." Her chill deepened, and she rubbed her hands up and down along her shins, trying to warm herself. "It was awful."

Dan moved to stand behind her, pressing his palms to her shoulders. Kelly relaxed at the warmth of his touch before she caught herself, shifting away from his contact. His move had been a stark reminder of Brian, comforting at a vulnerable moment.

She stood, pacing across the room away from him. She needed distance from the confusion he'd shaken to life deep within her.

"What did she look like?" Dan's words refocused her attention on their conversation.

"Elderly. White hair. Blue eyes. She was with a group. The aide, or whatever she was, apologized and led her away."

She pivoted to face him, avoiding eye contact. "The same thing happened today. They were out walking and she freaked out when she saw me."

Dan closed the space between them. Kelly lifted her gaze to his, all the while fighting the urge to look away, uncomfortable as the object of his scrutiny.

"You share some similar features, but the comparison stops there."

The rich undertones of Dan's voice sent heat scorching up Kelly's cheeks. His velvet eyes had darkened, and she wondered if he felt the same attraction she fought. Could he?

He suddenly pinched the bridge of his nose, any hint of desire vanishing from his expression. "Wait a minute. You said she was with a group?"

Kelly nodded. "Her name was Maddie."

"Maddie?" The word barely made it across Dan's lips before all color left his face. He pulled his wallet from a back pocket and slid out a single photograph. He handed it to Kelly.

In the snapshot, Dan stood with one arm around a pretty, young girl in a William and Mary sweatshirt. His other arm encircled the tiny woman with snow-white hair.

Kelly's breath caught and she raised her focus from the photo to Dan. "Your mother?" Her pulse roared in her ears.

He snatched his car keys from the table and reached for Kelly's hand. "Let's go."

Chapter Six

The smell was the first thing Kelly noticed as Dan buzzed them through the locked unit door. Sour and strong, it turned her stomach and she fought the urge to hold her nose. A woman's wail sent gooseflesh down her arms.

She turned to comment to Dan, but stopped when she saw the set of his jaw. This was how it must be each time he came to visit his mother. Kelly silently thanked Heaven her parents hadn't suffered this fate, even though their lives had ended far too soon. She pressed her hand to Dan's arm.

He stopped and turned toward her. "You okay?"

Kelly nodded, touched he'd asked. "You?"

"I'm used to this." His flat tone tugged at her heart. "Unfortunately."

He pushed open the door to a central room lined with tables and wheelchairs. A television blared from the corner of the room, playing a daytime drama for no one. Kelly followed Dan toward a bank of windows where a lone white-haired woman sat facing the marsh.

"Momma," Dan said softly. "I brought someone to meet you."

The woman sat motionless. A statue frozen by hands of time. "Candy Man," she mumbled.

Dan looked at Kelly and shook his head. "Might be a bad day," he mouthed.

He gestured to a chair and Kelly sank into it. She watched as he kneeled before his mother, gently brushing the hair from her forehead.

The gesture was at odds with the man Kelly thought Dan Steele to be. The gentle act hinted at emotional vulnerability—something he'd kept carefully guarded during the days she'd known him. Sure, she'd heard the pain in his voice anytime he'd spoken of Diane, but except for those few slips, he'd remained in control.

The older woman turned her gaze to her son, and Kelly swore her eyes softened, her face warming with color.

"Candy Man in the marsh," Maddie murmured.

"I know, Momma. I know." He took his mother's hands in his own. "My friend, Kelly, says she met you in the grocery store and near the post office. Do you remember meeting her?"

Maddie Steele turned toward Kelly. Kelly's pulse quickened as she watched a glimmer of recognition in the woman's pale eyes.

"He killed you," Maddie whispered.

Kelly's breath caught. She gripped the arms of the chair to steady herself.

"Who, Momma?" Dan asked. "Who killed her?"

"The Candy Man." Maddie returned her attention

to the window. "He plays in the marsh." She pulled one hand free from her son's grasp and pointed a frail finger toward the backwater of the sound. "He's there now."

Kelly jumped from her chair to lean against the windowsill. Dan stood next to her, scanning the area below.

"Where, Momma?"

Kelly scoured the marsh for any sign of movement, but saw nothing. Nothing but the sway of pines and grass in the autumn breeze.

"Right there," Maddie whispered. "The Candy Man."

Nothing. Nothing but the images of a woman's damaged mind. Kelly sagged with disappointment.

"There." Maddie's voice grew shrill. "There! He's killing her."

"Shh." Dan stroked his mother's cheek gently and patiently. "It's okay. He's gone now, Momma. Shh."

Kelly's heart twisted at the pain etched on Dan's face. Unlike the emotions she'd once watched Brian fake, Dan's expression shone with raw heartache.

Maddie returned her gaze to her son, a tear slipping from the corner of one eye. "No one believes me. No one cares."

"I care, Momma." He leaned and brushed his lips across his mother's forehead. "I always will."

"I'M SORRY we upset her like that," Kelly said as they crossed the parking lot toward Dan's car.

Dan hated that Kelly had witnessed his mother's illness up close and personal. He'd been a fool to bring her here. Some things were meant to be private among family.

"She won't remember." Frustration tinged his words. "That's even more cruel."

"How long has she been in assisted living?"

He shot a glance at Kelly's kind face, her expression set in what appeared to be genuine concern. No matter. He had no intention of letting her see any more of his secrets—or emotions.

"Too long."

Kelly's features fell at the sharp tone of his reply. He pressed his hand to the small of her back, the reflexive move at odds with his resolve to avoid letting this woman under his skin. Responding to her as anything other than a partner in a search for the truth would weaken him and his focus on nailing Miller. He needed distance from Kelly and the feelings she stirred inside him.

"I'll drop you at home." His voice sounded as though the visit had drained every ounce of his energy—as they usually did.

Kelly stopped, turning to face him. "I'm sorry for all you've been through."

Her dark brown eyes bore into Dan's. For a moment he longed to toss aside his need for distance and objectivity, wanting to lose himself in the comfort of her soft words. He bit back the urge to wrap his arms around her and hold on tight.

"I could use a cup of coffee. How about you?" Kelly's gentle gaze widened hopefully.

Dan caught his momentary lapse, snapping himself from the trance of temptation, reminding himself of their common bond. His sister and Rachel had both drowned with their bloodstreams full of the drug he'd helped bring to market.

He winced, remembering Diane's birthday. "I need to do something." An ominous bank of storm clouds encroached from the west, and Dan tipped his head toward the pitch-black horizon. "I'll get you home."

Kelly nodded, a forced smile turning up the corners of her lush mouth. "Sure. I understand."

Angry at herself for caring, Kelly fought the disappointment and frustration tangling her belly. She'd been so moved by Dan's gentle ways with his mother, she'd completely forgotten to keep her guard up. For several moments, her only thought had been to comfort him, to ease his apparent pain. She swallowed down the confusion choking her. Hadn't she learned enough with Brian? She'd be a fool to let Dan slip under her protective armor. A complete fool.

As they drove back toward Summer Shores from their visit with Maddie, Dan filled her in on his call from the pharmacy board.

She listened intently, but couldn't help asking the obvious. "What if you can't reach him again?"

A muscle tightened in Dan's jaw. "I will."

"Do you think your contact will know if Miller's telling the truth about the Pain Institute?"

Dan shot her a glance, his blue eyes gleaming with excitement. "I've got a plan for finding out ourselves."

The contrast between the fire in his eyes as he

spoke about Miller and the pain he'd shown back at the nursing home amazed Kelly. What if he was wrong? What if he was so desperate to clear his sister's name he'd conjured up a conspiracy where none existed?

Kelly sat back, choosing her words carefully. "What if you're wrong about all of this?"

Anger flashed in his glare. "You doubt me?"

Kelly raised a brow at his sharp tone. "I learned a long time ago to be cautious."

His eyes narrowed then refocused on the road ahead. Fat raindrops slapped against the windshield, heralding the arriving storm.

"Damn it," he swore under his breath.

"What's wrong?"

He visibly hesitated, as if it pained him to tell her his business. "Sometimes they close the cemetery if it storms."

The cemetery. Diane's birthday. How could she have forgotten?

She started to reach for his arm, but caught herself, steepling her fingers on her lap instead. "Go. I'll sit in the car. I'm not in a hurry to get home."

"Really?" he asked, and she nodded. His features eased as he pulled to the shoulder, made a U-turn and headed back toward the cemetery gates they'd passed a short while back.

HE WATCHED Steele head up the hill from his little sports car, no doubt going to visit his sister's burial spot. The girl stayed behind, sitting in the car with the windows cracked. The rain had slowed to a drizzle, but he figured Steele wouldn't stay long at the grave. He never did.

Fate had smiled on him once more when he'd spotted the Karmann Ghia making the U-turn along the highway. The sight of Kelly Weir riding in the passenger seat had been the icing on the cake.

Their little investigative liaison needed to be stopped. They'd teamed up quickly, picking up where Steele and Rachel had left off. The missing notes hadn't slowed them down one bit.

He had a bad gut feeling about the direction in which their investigation seemed to be headed. It was time their work came to a crashing halt.

He lined up Kelly's profile in the scope of the rifle. From this vantage point, she'd be an easy target, yet he'd be hidden from both the road and cemetery.

He laughed, catching himself before the sound traveled. A random shooting might draw some unwanted attention to Summer Shores, but he'd get away with it. Hell, the town was situated within an hour or two of several large cities.

He hated it when urban crime sprawled toward the coast.

He choked on another laugh as Kelly pushed open the passenger door and stood, heading into the cemetery.

Damn it. Now any shot would be almost impossible. He'd have to anticipate the maze of tombstones and mausoleums as she walked.

Fortunately, she didn't head in the same direction Steele had, probably to give him a measure of privacy. Wasn't that thoughtful of her. Too bad she hadn't been thoughtful enough to pack up Rachel's house and go home before she'd dug her nose into his business.

She paused in front of a small tombstone and sank to her knees. Perfect.

A clean shot.

He steadied his weapon, preparing to take out one more obstacle in his otherwise perfect plan. Suddenly, Steele appeared at the woman's side.

He pulled back, knowing a shot now would be stupid, as much as he wanted to pull the trigger. Anger seethed through him. Idiots. Why did they insist on their amateur investigation?

He clenched his jaw, fighting to keep his fury at bay. He couldn't. He needed a release. Now.

Aiming again, he steadied himself. It was time to teach them both a lesson.

DAN FOUGHT the sick sensation swirling through his gut. He hated this place. Hated that his sister's body lay here beneath the ground. A fresh wave of resolve spiraled out from his core. The pharmacy board or the institute would yield the clue he needed. They had to.

As he neared the car, his heart caught in his throat. The passenger seat sat empty.

Damn it. Hadn't Kelly said she'd wait in the car? What if Miller had followed them somehow? His anxiety flirted with panic until he turned and spotted her, kneeling partway up the hill in front of a grave.

He blew out a relieved breath as he headed for the spot.

"You ready to go?"

She lifted her watery gaze to his, and he frowned in confusion. Why the tears? Why here? His focus fell to the name on the tombstone. Yvonne Smithers. Another Oxygesic victim.

Guilt and self-loathing threatened to choke him. How many people had died because of the drug? The drug that had made his career. The career he'd chosen over a personal life.

"What if you're right about Miller being responsible?"

Kelly's voice jolted him to the present, sharpening his resolve. "I'll find a way to stop him."

An explosion cut through the damp afternoon. Dan instinctively dove for Kelly, pushing her to the ground just as the bark on a tree next to the tombstone exploded. A second shot rang out, and he wrapped his hand around her face, cradling her head as he pressed down on top of her, covering her body with his.

Silence followed, broken only by the hammering of Dan's heart against his ribs. An engine gunned. The shooter must be getting away.

Dan fought his urge to run, to follow, choosing instead to listen to his heart. He needed to make sure Kelly was safe and as far away from here as possible. He rolled off her, but took her hand, pulling her behind a large mausoleum.

Her damp hair clung to her cheeks and her neck. Fear shone brightly in her expression. All color had drained from her face.

"Are you hurt?" He scanned her from head to toe, searching for any sign she might have been hit by a bullet or flying debris.

Kelly shook her head, moisture gathering in her dark eyes. "What happened?"

Anger coursed through Dan's veins. "Someone shot at us…or you."

"Miller?"

He nodded. "I can't imagine who else."

Her throat worked as she struggled to assimilate what had just happened. Dan tugged her into his arms, gathering her close. Her body shook uncontrollably and he tightened his grip, wanting only to protect her from the danger he'd dragged her into.

"I've got you. You're all right."

He breathed the words against her cheek, and she nodded then pulled back to look into his eyes. Their gazes locked. The adrenaline slicing through Dan's veins took over. Without thought, he angled his mouth to hers, tasting her, drinking her in.

Raw fear and need battled inside him. Her sweet mouth welcomed his, her fingers tangling in the hair at the base of his skull.

She represented everything he'd fought against and fought for. The personal life—and love—he'd denied himself. The risk of heartache and loss. And now, she'd become the latest target of Miller's evil.

He broke the embrace, holding her at arm's length, his gaze dropping to her swollen lips. "I shouldn't have done that."

Kelly said nothing, only nodding, as if the shooting and his kiss had sucked the fight right out of her.

"I got caught up." He pulled her to her feet, brushing a blade of damp, cut grass from her cheek. "It won't happen again."

He led her quickly to the car, tucking her into the passenger seat and fastening her belt. He knelt beside her, pressing his palm flat to the damp material of her jeans.

"I'm not going to wait for the pharmacy board contact. I'm going straight to the institute."

The shocked look in Kelly's eyes faded, replaced with the familiar heat and fire of vitality. "I'm going with you."

Dan hesitated for a moment, battling the desire to send her packing back to Philadelphia, but things had changed since she'd arrived. The investigation had taken on a new urgency, and they'd obviously gotten too close for comfort, based on the attempted shooting.

"Fine." Dan stood and slammed the door, heading around the front of the car. He had no intention of extinguishing the determination in her eyes by telling her she could go with him to the institute, but she'd be waiting in the car.

THE NEXT AFTERNOON, Dan sat in the waiting room of Dr. Robinson's office, impatiently tapping his foot. He'd lucked out by landing an open appointment.

He scrubbed a hand across his exhausted eyes. He'd spent the night in Kelly's drive, keeping watch over her house. After he'd taken her home from the cemetery, Helen had agreed to stay with her, but he'd felt better being there, standing guard. He'd come back after the house grew dark and left just after dawn. She'd never known.

He'd called Jake, who'd promised to check out the tree in the cemetery, but had told Dan there had been drive-by shootings just north of Summer Shores in Norfolk that same day. He attributed the attempt on Kelly and Dan to nothing more than teenagers out for a thrill.

Dan squeezed his eyes shut and blew out an exasperated breath. What would it take for the detective to listen? Whatever it was, Dan vowed one thing. He wouldn't let Kelly become the victim who finally got Jake's attention.

She was probably going stir-crazy in the car right now. He'd thought about going back on his agreement to bring her, but had decided it was safest to keep a close eye on her. He wanted to keep Miller and Kelly far apart. The only way to do that was to keep tabs on her at all times.

Memories of their kiss had helped him stay awake all night. Never in his life had he been so drawn to a woman, and the attraction went far deeper than her physical appearance. Inside Kelly tangled an irresistible mix of pride, vulnerability, determination and heart. All Dan had to do now was fight any future urge to kiss her again.

A young man entered and approached the registration desk. College-aged, Dan guessed. The kid's sweatshirt hung loose over baggy jeans, his hair rumpled as if he hadn't showered in a few days. The appointment nurse waved him directly into the treatment area. Dan frowned. Must be a regular.

With that, Jake Arnold breezed through the door and gave the office manager a warm greeting. Dan snapped the magazine in his lap up in front of his face. He lowered it just enough to see over the top of the pages.

"Detective Arnold. We weren't expecting you today."

"I need to see the Doc for a minute," Jake said. "I screwed up and let my prescription run out. I called him. He's expecting me."

"Sure thing. Come on back."

Dan bristled at the ease with which Jake was granted access to the inner sanctum. Then he checked himself. What did he expect? Jake was a law enforcement officer and obviously a regular patient. Come to think of it, he had injured his back a while ago.

A few moments later, the young man emerged, exiting the waiting area without stopping at the desk. Jake followed a few seconds behind.

Dan slouched low in his chair, keeping the magazine in front of his face. The exit door had no sooner closed behind Jake than the nurse called out. "The doctor will see you now, Mr. Steele."

Dan's stomach tightened. Damn. That had been close. He'd have had one hell of a time explaining to Jake why he was here.

After waiting several more minutes in an exam room, Doctor Robinson entered. He seemed distracted as he questioned Dan about his injury.

As the good doctor jotted notes, Dan assessed his appearance. A large, gold nugget ring graced the pinkie of his left hand and what appeared to be a very expensive shirt and tie peeked out from the neck of his lab coat. Must be good money in pain management—or in writing phony prescriptions.

"You've noted that you pulled your back moving boxes." The doctor nodded. "Very common. One wrong move is all it takes." He clucked his tongue. "Were you lifting from your knees or your back?"

Dan shrugged. He hadn't thought the story that far through.

"Just as I thought." The doctor made a few notations in the chart then flashed a brilliant smile. "Probably a strain. Nothing more."

Dan grimaced. "I hope I haven't pinched a nerve. The pain is horrible." He forced a wince. "I haven't been able to sleep in days."

"Tell me what you've tried for relief."

"Ice, heat, ibuprofen, you name it."

Robinson nodded. "Well, I'd like to see you take it easy for a few days. Ice down at night and use moist heat in the morning." He pushed back on his stool and stood. "Come back in two weeks if there's no improvement."

"What about the pain?" Dan asked.

"Stick with the ibuprofen. There's no call for anything stronger at this point." He tucked the chart under his arm. "If the pain becomes intolerable, call the office." He stepped toward the door.

"I'm actually packing up the belongings of an ex-employee of yours." Dan's pulse quickened. Hell. While he was making things up, he might as well go for it.

Robinson slowly turned. "And whom might that be?"

"Rachel Braxton."

The doctor's eyes narrowed. "Ms. Braxton. Worked in Community Affairs, correct?" He clucked his tongue again. "Pity about her death."

"Did you know she had an opiate in her system when she drowned? Wonder if she got the drug here?"

The doctor's face flushed and he leveled a glare. "That's doubtful. Do they feel it was the cause of her death?"

"Apparently."

"It's misused in some instances." He shook his head. "It's an extremely effective drug that shouldn't be abused." Robinson pressed his lips into a tight line. "This is why I hesitate to prescribe painkillers unless I feel they're truly warranted. Good day, Mr. Steele. You know your way out?"

Dan nodded. Once Robinson left, he released the breath he'd been holding. Easing open the door, he stepped silently into the hall. Male voices sounded from around the corner. He froze in his tracks, listening.

"It's ready." Robinson's voice.

"Thanks," a second male voice mumbled. "See you next week."

With that a young man rounded the corner and slammed into Dan. A small square of paper fluttered to the floor. The stranger and Dan both fumbled to retrieve it.

"Sorry," the young man mumbled as they rammed shoulders.

"No problem." Dan straightened as the kid

plucked the slip from the carpet. He strained to read the notations scribbled on what appeared to be a prescription.

Dr. Robinson appeared, a severe scowl distorting his features. "Mr. Steele. Was there something else you needed?"

Urgency surged through Dan. He needed to see that paper. "No, Doctor. I must have gotten turned around."

Robinson pointed over Dan's shoulder. "The exit is behind you. Let me know if you have any problems once you've given that back a rest."

"Will do."

He stopped at the desk to pay his co-pay then hurried into the parking lot. The young man was nowhere in sight. There was only one thing to do.

Kelly sat waiting in the Karmann Ghia, arms crossed, still staring out the window. Too bad. He'd rather see her angry than hurt—or worse. Dan dropped into the driver's seat, cranked the ignition and sped out of the lot, headed straight for Miller's Apothecary.

If that prescription was going to be filled at Miller's, he planned to see exactly what it was.

Chapter Seven

Kelly watched from the greeting card aisle as Miller waited on the kid from the institute. At least Dan had let her come into the store alone. If Miller or the kid had seen Dan, all bets would have been off.

At first she'd been furious with Dan when he'd insisted she wait in the car at the institute. But, she'd wrangled her pride under control in light of the situation. She'd spotted his car in her drive when she'd been unable to sleep. He'd stayed all night, leaving just as daylight broke over the sound.

How could she be furious with a man who wanted to keep her safe?

They'd talked about the shooting again on the way to the doctor's office. She found it more than difficult to believe Detective Arnold had written it off, sight unseen, as a drive-by shooting.

She sucked in a deep breath to steady herself. She'd never been so afraid in her life, nor felt so safe as when Dan had encircled her in his strong embrace.

Neither of them had mentioned the kiss since it

had happened. The silence was probably for the best. Kelly had a strong sense that Dan was as conflicted by their deepening attraction as she was.

The young man handed over his prescription slip, and Kelly wrestled her attention from thoughts of Dan to the scene before her. He sank into a chair in the waiting area. Kelly slid farther into the card aisle, deciding to keep a low profile and follow him on his way out.

"Hey," a female voice said from behind her. "What are you doing hiding over here. Vince will be glad to see you."

Kelly's heart lurched. She turned to find Vince's assistant, Sarah, by her side.

"I needed a card," Kelly stammered. "I didn't want to bother Vince."

Sarah rolled her eyes. "He's nuts about you, let me tell ya. I'll tell him you're here."

"No, I—" Kelly reached for the young woman's sleeve, but she was gone. *Darn it all.*

Kelly continued to watch the young man, but slipped farther down the aisle, away from the pharmacy counter. She glanced up to find Sarah gesturing in her direction.

"Come on back. He's just got a few prescriptions to fill."

Kelly grimaced, returning the wave. Talk about blowing your cover. Dan would have her head once he found out she'd run smack into Miller.

"What a pleasant surprise. Going to take me up on my lunch offer after all?" Vince pulled Kelly into a bear hug. She pushed reflexively against his chest to free herself from his embrace and from his cloyingly sweet cologne. For all she knew, this man had tried to kill her less than twenty-four hours earlier.

"Actually…" Kelly waved the card she had hastily pulled from the rack "…I needed to pick up a card and some ibuprofen." Her heart jackhammered as she winced, holding the small of her back. "Hurt myself packing."

Vince counted tablets into the slot of a tray then dumped them into a vial. He pulled a label from a printer and expertly smoothed it onto the plastic container.

"Should have called me." He turned to Kelly, his smile sending a shudder across her shoulders. "For you, I'd make house calls." He handed her a bottle.

Kelly's gaze dropped to the label. Ibuprofen. Probably laced with strychnine.

"On the house." Vince drew the last word into a hiss.

"This wasn't necessary, but thanks." Kelly stepped toward the lab door. "I should go. You're trying to work."

"Stay. I'll rub your back."

He leaned across the counter and nodded to the young man Kelly had been following. The kid stepped to the counter, holding out several bills.

Vince took the cash and made change from his pocket without uttering a word.

A cash sale? From his *pocket?* Adrenaline pumped through Kelly's veins. Perhaps she and Dan finally had the break they needed. She glanced nervously at the departing man's back. She had to move quickly.

"Listen, Vince." She stepped from the threshold of the half door into the main section of the store. "I need to get going. I just thought of something I forgot to do."

"Dinner later?" His ice-blue gaze widened hopefully.

"Maybe." At that point she'd promise him just about anything to end the conversation and get out the door.

"It would be nice to spend some time with someone from home."

Kelly stopped, turning back to face him. "From home?"

"You're from Philly, right?" He patted his chest. "I'm from Jersey. I'd love to hear what's new up North."

"I didn't know you were from New Jersey." *Too close for comfort.* Her pulse pounded in her ears. "How long have you lived here?"

He shrugged. "A few years. I was due for a change of scenery."

"Can't blame you." She waved goodbye, hurrying toward the front door. "Thanks for the ibuprofen."

"I'd love to get some pictures of you sometime, Kelly. For my portfolio."

His words trailed behind, chilling her to the bone.

"I'm not very photogenic," she called out over her shoulder.

"Everyone's photogenic. Everyone." He spoke the words robotically, methodically. Kelly shook off her nerves as she pushed out into the fresh air.

The young man stood unlocking the door to a battered Chevy Nova.

"Didn't I just see you over at the Pain Institute?" Kelly called out.

He looked up at her, his gaze narrowing. "I think I'd remember you."

"Well." Kelly pasted on her warmest smile. "I remember you." She shrugged, hoping she looked nonchalant.

He pulled open the door and slid onto the seat, obviously not interested in striking up a conversation with some nosy woman in a parking lot.

"Seriously, didn't you see Doctor Robinson?" Kelly stepped next to the Nova, making sure to show plenty of leg. "I'm just wondering what you think of him. He wants me to try exercise before he gives me anything for the pain. How about you?"

The young man's gaze trailed up the length of Kelly's leg. At least something had gotten his attention. He lifted his green eyes to meet hers. "Football injury. Needed a refill slip for my prescription." His car's engine chugged to life and he reached to pull his door shut. Kelly stood her ground.

"Do you go to school down here?"

He shook his head. "Norfolk Community."

"That's a long drive, isn't it?"

"The institute's the best place around." He smiled. "Good care, you know?"

Kelly nodded. "Do you mind me asking what he gives you?"

"Oxygesic." He winked. "Really does the trick."

"I'll remember that."

Kelly stepped clear of his door. He pulled it shut and sped out of the parking lot. As she turned toward the street, she caught a glimpse of movement in the pharmacy window. Someone in white. A lab coat, perhaps.

Her stomach pitched, and pinpricks of dread crept up her neck as she hurried for Dan's car.

DAN PULLED the slip of paper from his wallet while he waited for Kelly, keeping the apothecary's entrance in the rearview mirror.

He punched the phone number into his cell and pushed Send. Scott Jansen answered on the third ring, but fell silent after Dan identified himself.

"You don't have to say a word. Just give me one minute of your time. That's all I ask."

Silence.

"Rachel was a friend of mine and I know she was investigating the misuse of Oxygesic in this region. I also know she was investigating Miller's Apothecary specifically. What I need to know is if you have any hard data there that could be used as evidence against Miller."

Silence.

Dan rubbed the bridge of his nose. If the guy didn't say something soon, his controlled reserve was about to spill over. "Miller says his distribution level is acceptable because he's the only pharmacy in the area that carries Oxygesic. Something about theft possibilities and—"

"He's lying." Jansen's voice filtered across the line, nothing more than a gruff whisper.

"What?" Dan leaned into the phone, his heart tapping against his chest. "He's lying about what?"

"I'll meet you. Day after tomorrow. There's an Applebee's partway between Summer Shores and Carrboro. Rocky Mount. 301 Bypass. Eleven o'clock."

"And you've got proof?"

The line clicked dead. Dan scrambled for a pen in the glove box.

Two days.

He was going to take down Miller for his role in the illegal Oxygesic market. He'd expose the truth behind both Diane and Rachel's deaths and the attack on Kelly.

The now familiar protectiveness swelled inside him. Dan had put Kelly in harm's way because of his need for the truth, just as he'd done with Rachel.

But this time, the end result would be different. If it were the last thing he did, Dan would take Miller out of commission before he could hurt anyone ever again.

KELLY TOOK a long sip of the merlot Dan had poured. She appeared small, her legs curled up beneath her as she sat on his sofa.

Hot anger boiled inside him, threatening to break through his wall of control. "From now on, we're keeping you far away from Miller."

She studied him with bright eyes, dark circles smudging the pale skin just beneath her lashes. She said nothing, the emotional and physical toll of the past few days starkly visible in her weary expression.

Dan dropped next to her on the sofa, taking her hand in his. She yielded to his touch, though her fingers tensed beneath his.

She'd already told him everything that had happened at Miller's. He'd summarized his conversation with Jansen, and now they sat in silence as Kelly visually inspected the interior of Dan's oceanfront home. He'd brought her here on instinct, not wanting her to be home alone.

"You never gave me a straight answer on what you do for a living." Incredulity tinged her words.

"Did," he replied, anxiety building over the direction the conversation had taken. Should he come clean? Should he tell her he owed his early retirement and comfortable lifestyle to stock options granted as his reward for the multibillion dollar success of Oxygesic? No.

"I had a good career." He spoke the words curtly, hoping to dissuade additional questions. "Now I do some consulting. Let's leave it at that."

Her fingers relaxed beneath his, interlacing with his as she turned her palm over.

Dan's insides hummed to life, heat uncoiling from deep in his core. Touching Kelly had been a mistake. His heart twisted and he mentally scolded himself. There was no room for desire or weakness in his life. He had to keep his attention on Miller. They were too close to the truth to risk a misstep now.

He pulled his hand free from hers. "About yesterday."

Kelly straightened, shaking her auburn waves. "You don't need to say it." A shadow passed across her dark eyes as she continued. "Your concern for me is obviously real, but I also see the fire of your determination. It's what drives you. Let's not confuse whatever this is that's happening between us with anything other than what it is. I'm a means to your end."

She might as well have slapped him, but she was right. He couldn't have said it better himself. Putting a stop to their growing attraction was for the best. "We understand each other then," he said. "I'll drive you home."

She stood, stepping away from the sofa. When she turned back to face him, Dan started at the pain painted across her lovely features.

He unfurled himself from the sofa. "What aren't you telling me?"

Kelly blinked, apparently surprised she'd been that transparent. "His name was Brian." She hoisted her chin, meeting Dan's scrutiny head-on. "Let's leave it at that."

He studied her proud posture, admiring her resolve. She'd obviously been hurt in the past, but it was none of his business. Curiosity about her personal life could only weaken his focus, and he had no intention of letting that happen.

"Fair enough." He nodded toward the door. "Let's go."

KELLY'S HEART sat heavy in her stomach on the way back to her house. Silence hung awkwardly between her and Dan as she stared out the passenger window. His agreement had told her all she needed to know.

She *was* only a means to an end, as she'd been to Brian.

Sadness welled inside her. The feelings she'd begun to harbor for Dan were a mistake—a horrible mistake.

It had been so long since she'd wanted to make love, since she'd trusted someone enough to offer her body. Yet, today, for a split second when she'd intertwined her fingers with Dan's—when she'd seen what she thought was genuine caring shining in his gaze—she'd wanted to lower her defenses. She'd wanted to offer her heart to him. He'd made her feel safe. Protected and cared for.

Kelly stole a glance at his profile. A hint of gray tipped the hair just above his ears. The reflected light from outside the car caught the angles of his face, the line of his jaw. Her insides squirmed and she shifted in her seat.

Thank goodness he'd made it clear exactly where they stood before she'd done something she'd regret forever.

Her sole focus now should be on working alongside Dan to solve the mystery behind Rachel's death. Kelly might have failed Rachel by being unforgiving in life, but she could try to make amends now. Perhaps somewhere out there Rachel would know.

A few moments later, as she and Dan climbed the steps to the front door, a sliver of white caught Kelly's eye. An envelope sat propped against the door and she bent to pick it up.

"Secret admirer?" Dan slipped her key into the lock, pushing the door open as she pulled a greeting card from the envelope. Her heart lodged in her throat. The card from Miller's store. She'd left it on the pharmacy counter.

"Miller's been here." She looked up at Dan, his worried gaze meeting hers.

"What does it say?"

She shook her head. "Nothing. I told him I needed to buy this and then I left it there." She winced, mentally berating herself. "How stupid."

"Come on. Get inside."

His palm pressed against the small of her back, easing her through the door then steering her toward the sofa. "I'll check the house."

She stared at the card in her hand, shivering. Dan's footsteps echoed against the hardwood floor as he made his way through the house and the lower level.

She ran her finger over the flap of the envelope. Had this been left for her by a killer? Had Miller murdered Rachel? Diane? Had he taken the shot in the cemetery? Was she his newest target?

Dan reappeared at the top of the steps, his features tense with concern. "No sign of anyone getting in. You're good." He dropped next to her on the sofa, tenderly cupping her chin in his palm. "Look at me."

She fought the tears welling in her eyes. She wasn't weak. She *would not* cry.

"I won't let anything happen to you." Determination filled Dan's voice, the planes and angles of his face taut and serious. He spoke softly, as if soothing a frightened child. "I got you into this."

Kelly shook her head, emotion swirling through her from both Miller's calling card and the warmth of Dan's fingers cradling her chin. "No. I needed to do this for Rachel." Her memory deserved for the truth to be revealed.

"But I involved you."

His spicy scent enveloped her, dulling her focus. She resisted the urge to press closer, concentrating instead on Miller and the threat he represented.

Miller's parting words about New Jersey echoed through her brain. "Miller said he was from New Jersey." Her pulse quickened. "There's a reporter back home I want to call."

"Why?" Dan's hand dropped away from her face, leaving the skin chilled where his fingers had rested.

Kelly dropped the card onto the coffee table, bolstered by her idea. "He might know something about Miller's past."

The thought of Miller having been on her porch, at her door, sent tremors through her body. If he'd done this before, at home, in New Jersey, she wanted to know. In the meantime, she did *not* want to be alone tonight—not in this house.

She measured the tense expression on Dan's face, battling her desire to ask him to stay. She wanted him inside the house, where his presence would ease the fear swirling inside her. She lowered her head, searching for the right words. "Dan, I—"

"I'm staying." He stood and paced the small living room floor. "It's too risky for you to be by yourself." He shoved a hand through his close-cropped waves. "I'll sleep on the sofa."

Relief flooded through Kelly. "Deal."

"No argument?"

She shook her head. "None. I'll put some towels in the bathroom and find a blanket for you." She stopped partway down the hall. "You know, you could use the spare bedroom."

Dan frowned, jerking his thumb toward the front door. "I'd rather be right here in case our friend comes back."

The blinking red light of the answering machine caught Kelly's eye as she stepped into the bedroom. She pressed the Play button then opened the closet door to gather linens for Dan. Her hand froze on the doorknob when she heard Miller's voice.

"Kelly." His recorded voice sent the small hairs at the back of her neck bristling to attention. "I'm sorry you were in such a hurry today. We never get to spend enough time together. That's going to have to change."

Several seconds of dead air played out before he spoke again. "You forgot your card. I left it at your front door. I'm sure it was an honest oversight."

More dead air.

"I'll see you soon, Kelly. Very soon."

The beep of the machine signaled the end of the recording. Kelly's hand remained gripped to the doorknob, and she struggled to find her breath.

"DAMN IT." Dan brought his fist down hard against the desktop. "I don't want this guy after you." He spun to face Kelly. She'd gone pale, appearing small, wrapped in the afghan he'd draped around her shoulders. "I'm doing this alone from here on out."

Stubborness flashed in her eyes. "No, you're not.

If you think I'm letting him scare me off, you're sadly mistaken."

Dan stepped back, anger twisting his insides into knots. "Scare you off? Kelly, the man may be out to kill you."

Kelly pulled herself up from the bed and stepped to where he stood. Toe to toe, she pressed her finger to his chest. "You think I'm some weak female you need to protect. I can hold my own." She shuddered, her body belying her tough talk.

Dan reached to pull the soft wrap back into place, letting his hand linger longer than he needed to, fighting the urge to pull her into his arms.

"I won't do anything stupid."

The soft glow of the nightstand lamp lit shimmers of red in her hair. Her eyes glistened, wide and bright, her cheeks flushed with determination. *Beautiful.* She was the most beautiful thing Dan had ever set eyes on.

"Two women have already died. I'll do whatever it takes to make sure you're not the third." He realized then that he'd lied back at his house when he'd agreed with her dismissal of their growing connection. No matter what his head thought, his heart knew better. "I care about you, Kelly. You're far more than a means to an end."

She took a step back, the pink of her cheeks deepening. He closed the space between them, running his thumb down her cheek, then letting his hand fall to his side. He stepped back, startled by the depths of his own emotions.

He wanted her so badly he ached. And now she

knew it. After all, she wasn't stupid. "I'll be on the sofa."

He turned, quickly heading for the living room before his tenuous control slipped any more than it already had.

KELLY LAY awake, staring at the ceiling. *I'll be on the sofa.* Dan's words bounced around her brain, tangling with her own inner turmoil. Sleep eluded her. Even though exhaustion seeped through her bones from her lack of sleep the night before, she couldn't quiet her thoughts.

She wanted to believe he did care. She wanted to believe he slept on her sofa out of concern for her safety and not a fear of missing a vital clue. But the specter of Brian whispered at the back of her brain.

Brian had been kind, loving, caring, yet all the while he'd been copying her files and documents, forging her signature, setting her up to fail. All to better his own career. She'd known him for two years and had been fooled. Why did she feel so compelled to trust the virtual stranger asleep down the hall?

Kelly slipped out of bed, wondering if Dan's thoughts were as tormented as hers. Soft snoring filtered from the living room. Well, at least one of them was able to sleep.

His head hung over the edge of the sofa and his arm lay draped on the floor. Lord, he wouldn't be able to move at all in the morning.

Even asleep, he emitted a quiet intensity, as if he held all of his emotions just below the surface, fighting to keep control. He'd slipped earlier, allowing her a glimpse of the passion inside. She wondered just what would happen if he was ever careless enough to let his raw need escape unchecked.

She kneeled next to him, gingerly repositioning the pillow beneath his head. She worked to slide his upper body toward the inside of the sofa, holding her breath as he stirred. She didn't want to wake him.

In a blur of movement, he tightened his arm around her back, pulling her against his chest so quickly Kelly had no time to react. His mouth found hers and she struggled momentarily then relaxed into the feel of his lips pressed against her own.

Shock waves of need spiked through her. His caress was sensual, tender and all she'd dreamed of. She softened against him, trailing her fingertips along his cheek.

He pulled his lips from hers and whispered, "Did you need me?"

"More than you know."

He trailed hot, hungry kisses down her neck, and a moan escaped from somewhere deep inside her.

Dan had thought Kelly would never weaken, and he'd been determined not to make the first move. He knew she desired him as much as he wanted her. It had been written in the gentleness of her touch and in the fire of her gaze.

He had just dozed off when her movements had roused him—then aroused him.

Her mouth was ravenous and wanting on his, her warm, sweet breath mingling with his own. Her hair fell in a sexy tangle of strands over his face.

Dan stroked a palm across the swell of her breast

and heard her moan again. Need pulsed through him for the woman he had vowed not to care about, yet she'd become the center of each day—the first thing he thought of upon awakening and the last face to float through his mind each night.

At times stubborn and maddening, she was also kind, compassionate and more intriguing than anyone he'd ever known.

He wanted to make her feel pleasure like she'd never felt before. He wanted to erase the fears and doubts this Brian person had obviously left buried inside her. He wanted to keep her safe.

His thoughts terrified him, and he broke their kiss.

He gazed into her beautiful face, lit softly by the night sky filtering in through the window. If they made love they'd be crossing a line. *A big line.*

Was he ready to make love to her? To risk the pain that could follow? The memories of his mother's grief-stricken sobs haunted him.

"Are you all right?" Kelly's whisper tumbled over her soft, swollen lips, her features radiant, inviting, irresistible.

His pulse quickened, her words of concern ratcheting up his need. Several of her lush, auburn locks fell softly about the pale skin of her shoulders, and a fresh jolt of desire pulsed through him.

She brought her lips within a hairsbreadth of his and whispered, "Dan?"

He touched a finger to her lips. "Too much talking."

He slid the straps of her nightgown from her shoulders, brushing the tips of his fingers across her satiny skin. She closed her eyes, her tongue moistening her lower lip. Dan pressed a kiss to the hollow of her neck and her body responded, arching toward him. His desire snaked and coiled within him, clamoring for release.

He pulled her onto his lap, easing her nightgown down over her breasts. He longed to taste her, gently suckling a nipple and the surrounding flesh into his mouth. He flicked his tongue across her tender skin—teasing, tasting.

Kelly's hands caressed him, slipping slowly, tortuously along his sides. Hot need scorched through his veins, filling him with a frenzied assurance that making love to Kelly was anything but wrong.

He fingered the hem of her nightgown, working it higher along her creamy thigh until he hooked the satin of her panties. She leaned back, granting him access to her moist, hot desire. He slipped a finger inside, slowly stroking, savoring the sound of her breath, coming now in shallow pants.

Dan intended to make love to her fully and completely like she'd never been made love to before.

Kelly rocked with the motion of his touch, cupping her breast into his hungry mouth. He slipped his palms to her hips, easing from beneath her. Her long fingers stroked through the fabric of his boxers as he grappled on the floor for his jeans.

Relief surged through him when his fingertips found the foil packet tucked inside his wallet. What little control he had left was about to explode.

Kelly chased the shadow of doubt from her mind as Dan sheathed himself. The intensity of her desire had sent her head reeling, not to mention the havoc it had wreaked on her body. Determined not to doubt or think, she silently vowed only to *feel*.

Dan's fingers slipped her legs free of her panties and guided her on top of him. He entered her gently, and she shuddered at the sensation of being filled so completely. Like a dream, she could barely believe they were together. Joined as one.

He gripped her waist, easing her into a slow, sensual dance, their bodies moving to a shared rhythm of desire.

Mind-blowing sensations built within her, threatening to crescendo and explode. Sudden panic rippled through her and she slowed. Was she ready to give herself to this man? A man she trusted, no matter how hard she'd tried not to.

"Kelly," Dan whispered.

Her name on his lips washed away the anxiety. *Don't think. Just feel.*

She focused on the heat of his skin against hers, on the gentle touch of his palms against her flesh, on the agonizingly intense sensations of pleasure he'd fired within her.

And suddenly she was lost. Lost in a fog of surrender and desire. Of lust and need.

Dan gripped her buttocks, thrusting fully into her. The force of his move shocked her, thrilled her. She gasped as release splintered through her, carrying her over the edge.

Dan's eyes drifted closed, a groan ripping from deep inside him as his own orgasm pulsed through his body. They moved as one. Rocking. Releasing. Loving.

When Kelly fell limp against his chest, Dan brushed the hair from her neck, nuzzling his lips to her cheek before he pulled her down for a long, deep kiss.

HE SAT down the street, waiting for Steele's car to leave. By three o'clock in the morning, he realized tonight was not going to be his night.

He'd lost control when he'd taken the shots at the cemetery. He didn't like it when he lost control. It wouldn't happen again.

Next time, he'd be more careful. More methodical.

He twisted the ignition key, listening to the engine turn over, a blast of power against the quiet ocean breeze. His power.

He eased the car away from the curb, knowing next time there'd be no mistakes.

Chapter Eight

The phone woke Kelly shortly after seven.

She glanced over the rumpled covers at Dan's dark hair peeking from beneath the sheets. She warmed with a glimpse of his bare shoulder and relaxed expression. He actually looked peaceful. She hadn't thought it possible.

As much as she'd fought it, Kelly cared for this man. Deeply. While their emotional connection had been tenuous ever since they'd met, making love had been seamless, as if they'd been made for each other.

A shiver of dread danced along her spine and she slapped it away, hoping Dan had spoken the truth when he'd told her what she meant to him. When he'd explained she meant far more to him than a means to an end.

Kelly dragged her attention away from Dan, pulling the receiver close to her mouth and forcing out her groggy voice. "Hello."

"Kelly, it's Vince."

She came awake in an instant, trepidation rippling through her. "Vince."

Dan pushed himself up from his pillow, frowning. He reached for the phone, but Kelly turned her back.

"I'm sorry to call you so early, but I wanted to make sure you got your card."

Kelly shivered. "I did. Thank you."

"Where were you?"

"I was out with a friend."

"A friend?" He paused for a beat, and Kelly's breath caught. She didn't want to set him off. "I didn't know you had friends down here."

She thought quickly. "From college. She stopped by and we went out for a late dinner. No big deal." She fought to keep her voice calm, fervently hoping he'd believe her lie.

"O-kay." He drew the word into two syllables. "Just wanted to make sure you were all right. I was surprised you weren't there. After all, I had mentioned dinner."

Kelly winced. "I'm sorry. I completely forgot."

"Another time perhaps."

"Perhaps." Not if she could help it. Just hearing the man's voice set her teeth on edge. "Thanks for calling, Vince. I'll talk to you later."

Kelly hung up quickly and turned to Dan. He had pulled on his jeans and stood watching her, hands on his hips, brows furrowed. His peaceful expression had been replaced by the familiar determined intensity.

"Is it too early to call your reporter friend?"

Kelly shook her head. Dan closed the space between them, reached for her chin, but then lowered his hand to his side without touching her.

Kelly blinked, taken aback by the detached stance he assumed. No one would ever guess at the level of intimacy they'd shared last night.

Dan shrugged into his shirt. "Make the call. I'll start some coffee." He pivoted sharply, disappearing down the hall.

She stared at the empty threshold for several long seconds. Had Dan already begun to regret letting her behind his protective wall? Or had she misjudged him? Misread him?

Maybe their night of lovemaking had been nothing more than two people clinging to each other after their brush with death. She shivered. Maybe he was just using her after all.

DAN POURED himself a steaming cup of coffee, trying to eavesdrop on Kelly's conversation. She'd reached Rick DeSanto on the first try, and it sounded as though the reporter had plenty of information on Vince Miller.

Miller had certainly given Dan a wake-up call—literally. Dan had let himself relax, losing himself in the sheer indulgence of Kelly's body. He'd lost focus and let down his guard. Miller's call served as a grim reminder that one slip on Dan's part could lead to disaster.

Dan hadn't been sharp enough to save Rachel. He wouldn't make the same mistake with Kelly, but if he let his heart get entangled with hers, he'd lose all objectivity. Who was he kidding? His heart was already entangled. Making love had been a mistake in judgment, but he wouldn't let it happen again.

He downed his second cup of coffee just as Kelly rounded the corner.

"Miller threatened a woman back home." Her tone had gone tight. "He relocated here after the story hit the paper. He sold his chain of stores and bailed."

Dan frowned. "How could he just leave?"

"The woman he'd stalked and threatened just wanted him out of her life. Two others came forward, but no charges were ever filed. They were happy he'd left town."

Dan's thoughts tossed and tumbled, whirling through his brain like a dust storm. "Any Oxygesic dealings up there?"

Kelly shook her head. "Apparently nothing out of the ordinary. His thing was photos."

A vision of the shots Kelly had been working on flashed through Dan's mind. "Photos?"

Kelly nodded. "He used them as calling cards. Calling cards with threatening messages."

Dan stiffened. Miller had harassed his sister and Rachel. Who knew what other women he'd stalked, or worse. He set his empty mug on the counter with a thunk. "I've got to go."

He brushed past Kelly without so much as a sideways glance, focused on confronting Jake Arnold about this latest information. If Miller had come to Summer Shores with an unsavory past, why in the hell hadn't anyone been told about it?

Had Jake let a suspected criminal move into town to set up shop? Why?

Dan paused at the door, turning back. Kelly stood

where he'd left her, her face twisted with a mix of confusion and fear. He took a step toward her, intent on offering comfort, but then decided against it.

They'd both be better off if they went forward as if last night had never happened. As he stomped down the outside steps he mentally berated himself. Making love to Kelly was one line he should have never crossed.

The clues weren't only pointing to Miller, they were flashing in big, bold neon letters. Big bold letters with an arrow pointing straight at Kelly—as Miller's next target. Dan would do whatever it took to make sure this time Miller didn't hit his mark.

LATER THAT NIGHT, Kelly and Dan drove in silence as they headed toward Norfolk Community College. Jake had refused to see him, and Dan's anger and frustration filled the small car.

Kelly blurted out her thoughts when she could no longer take the quiet. "Can't we push this? Go over his head? Something."

Dan's profile tensed, a muscle pulsing in his jaw. "We'd be wasting our time."

Impatience built inside Kelly. "But he's a detective, for crying out loud. You'd think he'd want to keep an eye on Miller. Does he even care about his past?"

"He told me he cares," Dan said flatly. "And he watches."

Kelly fell silent at the intensity of Dan's tone, biting her lip to keep back the annoyance ready to bubble over.

After another long, uncomfortable silence, Dan pulled the car into a lot outside what promised to be a crowded pub. College students poured down a narrow set of concrete steps leading to the entrance.

Kelly reached for her door, but Dan caught her other hand and gave it a squeeze, the first affectionate move he'd made since their awkward parting that morning. The contact ignited heat and hope, low and heavy within her.

"Miller gave my sister some trouble. He backed off pretty quickly when he realized she was involved with Jake. He also harassed Rachel." Dan shook his head. "I'm not sure how quickly he backed off of that one. If he ever did."

"Helen told me about Rachel."

Dan nodded, releasing what sounded like a very frustrated breath as he let go of her hand. She eyed him carefully, trying to decide whether or not to ask about the one thing that didn't add up.

"Why would Jake let Miller stay in Summer Shores?" Kelly frowned, leaning close. "Especially after he'd harassed Diane and Rachel. Isn't that asking for trouble?"

Dan shrugged. "Miller had no official charges against him in New Jersey. All Arnold could do was keep an eye on him."

"And now Miller's branched out into dealing prescription drugs."

Dan's gaze locked with hers, the fire in his look drawing her irresistibly toward him. "That's what you and I are going to prove."

Kelly reached out, running her finger along the

sharp line of his jaw. He captured her hand in his. Her heart tattooed against her ribs as his focus dropped to her mouth.

"Last night can't happen again." His voice had gone thick, husky.

Kelly swallowed down the need that choked her throat, tightening her from the inside out, like a coil that was about to spring.

"I plan to keep you safe. I can't do that if I'm distracted."

Dan pushed open his driver's door, unfurling himself from the car. Kelly climbed from the passenger seat, grabbing his elbow as he headed for the pub steps.

"If Jake was involved with your sister, why isn't he pursuing this like you are?"

Dan turned to her, his eyes softening. "Because he loved her. What if he screwed up? Maybe he can't live with the possibility he might have missed the one thing that could have saved her. Maybe it's easier to believe she overdosed and drowned."

Kelly couldn't help but wonder if the words he spoke didn't apply to himself, as well. "And you?"

Dan pulled his elbow from her grip, leaning close. "I'm not Jake." He shot her a look so potent it rocked her to her core. "Let's go."

Her emotions battled as she followed him down the dark staircase. She wanted so badly to let this man under her skin, wanted to believe he was nothing like Brian. But would that leap of faith be her biggest mistake yet?

Dan took her hand as they eased into the crowded

space, his fingers intertwining with hers. The intimacy of his touch sent her pulse racing. One thing was for sure. As much as she wanted to deny it, Dan Steele had made one heck of an impression on her heart.

The air in the bar was warm and close, the sour smell of spilled beer bringing back memories of Kelly's own college days. Music thumped from a dark corner of the dance floor where a small band huddled on an elevated stage.

Dan squeezed her hand. "I think we should split up," he yelled, fighting to be heard above the din. "You okay with that?"

She nodded, giving him the thumbs-up, then watching him disappear into the crowd of bodies filling the small space. She turned toward the bar and walked smack into the young man from Miller's.

"You following me?" he yelled.

Kelly's heart jumped to her throat. She shook her head. "I came in for a drink."

"Right." He gave her a sly grin and a wink, nodding to the opposite corner of the bar. "I spotted you as soon as you came in. Come on. It's easier to talk over there."

Kelly's pulse roared in her ears, competing with the beat of the music. She glanced frantically over her shoulder, but Dan was nowhere in sight. She followed the young man into a narrow hallway, where he'd stopped beneath a crooked restroom sign.

"Look, if you wanted some stuff, you should have just said so yesterday. You didn't need to track me down."

Kelly narrowed her eyes. "Stuff?"

The kid laughed then paused for a beat. "You're kidding me, right?" He leaned toward her. "You want to get high. That's why you had all the questions about Oxy."

His stale breath brushed across Kelly's face, turning her stomach. She took a step backward, working to steady herself.

"What if I did want some stuff? Are you the guy to see?"

He shook his head. "No, lady. I'm this week's runner. Nothing more." He patted her shoulder and she fought the urge to cringe beneath his touch. "You're too late anyway. Everyone knows the goods are sold out by now."

"Why are you telling me all this?"

He shrugged a bony shoulder. "You look like you've got money. We can always use another well-paying client."

"We?"

He winked. "You ask too many questions." His smile suddenly slipped into a frown as he stepped back. "Hey. You're not a reporter or something, are you? They told us to watch out for reporters."

"They?"

"Nice try." He drained his beer, tossing the bottle into a trashcan. "We're through talking. Forget what I said."

Kelly grabbed for his arm as he brushed past, hooking his elbow. "Who are you running for? Miller?"

He pulled free of her grip, scowling. "You should

leave now." The air seemed to still. Kelly held her breath. "And you might want to watch your back."

Kelly stood stunned as he slipped away, merging into the swaying crowd. She wrapped her arms around her waist to fight the trembling spreading from deep inside her, not sure if she was scared of the kid, or of who he might rat her out to.

DAN SPOTTED THEM from across the room. Kelly had a grip on some kid's arm, and the kid did not look happy. Excusing himself, Dan pressed between two young women, pushing them out of the way.

So much for the old days. He hadn't been able to strike up a single conversation, other than the one where the young woman asked him if his son looked anything like him. He wasn't even forty yet, for crying out loud.

The young man pulled away from Kelly and disappeared into the crowd. She stood alone, a dazed look on her face.

"Hey." He took her shoulders in his hands and gave her a quick shake. "You okay?"

"Let's get out of here."

He slipped an arm around her waist, pulling her close. They forced their way through the crowd and up the steps to the outside. The cool autumn air was a welcome relief from the stifling space below.

"What happened?"

"That's the kid I talked to at Miller's."

"Whoa. You sure as hell had better luck than I did."

She stood next to the passenger door, her eyes

wide and full of fear. "Not if he describes me to Miller. Can we go? He gave me the creeps."

Damn, she was right. If the kid went straight to Miller, who knew what he'd do. Kelly shuddered and he pulled her into his arms.

He tucked her head beneath his chin, his heart squeezing at the feel of her trembling within his embrace. He'd pulled her right into danger when her only mission in Summer Shores had been to pack up her friend's life. "I'm sorry."

Kelly nodded against his chest, shivering as he brushed his hand across her back.

It took every ounce of restraint he possessed not to kiss her, but right now that wasn't what Kelly needed. What she needed was for Dan to nail Miller once and for all.

THE HOUSE STOOD DARK. Kelly's Jetta sat parked in the drive, but there was no sign of life behind the windows. He pressed the button on his watch to illuminate the face. Twelve-fifteen. Good enough.

The full moon cast a pale ivory glow across the yard as he followed the edge of the house to the back staircase, carefully climbing the wooden steps. He hesitated at the top, scrutinizing the bedroom doors. The blinds had been left open and no lights shone inside.

He crossed the deck without a noise then tried the handle on the French doors. Locked. He slipped a credit card from his wallet and slid it deftly next to the doorknob, popping the lock. So much for security.

He stepped inside, pausing to let his eyes adjust. Soft shadows filtered through the panes of glass and onto the bedspread. He lowered himself to the edge of the bed, flipping back the covers. He hoisted a pillow to hold it to his face. Fresh. Clean. Interfering.

Dropping the pillow, he crossed to the computer, running his gloved fingers across the surface. Notes and papers lay scattered across the desktop. He pulled the eight-by-ten glossy print from the zippered front of his jacket, pausing to admire it once more.

In the photo, Kelly lay sleeping in a tangle of sheets, her smooth thigh exposed, one arm dangling from the side of the bed. In neat black printing on a white label, he had typed, *I came to see you and you weren't here. I don't like that.*

He put a hand over his mouth to muffle his laugh, propping the photo against the computer monitor. He stepped back to admire his work, nodding with satisfaction.

Maybe this would cure her curiosity about Rachel Braxton and Oxygesic. Something had to.

He pulled a candy out of his jacket pocket and peeled off the wrapper. Grape. Shoving the wrapper into the pocket of his jeans, he turned to leave, locking the French door on his way out. You couldn't be too careful, after all.

KELLY WRAPPED her arms around her waist, waiting in the living room as Dan checked the house. She'd agreed to let him spend the night again. The thought soothed her raw nerves, but she wasn't sure she could trust her heart to another night of lovemaking. If he stayed, that's exactly where they'd be headed.

No matter what he'd said about last night being a mistake, she had no doubt he was as conflicted emotionally as she was, if not more.

She sank onto the sofa, leaning her heavy head against the back of the seat. The last few days were catching up. Rachel. Miller. Dan.

She'd become exhausted physically and emotionally. Perhaps she should pack up and leave. No one would blame her. Her life could be in danger. Hell, her life was in danger. Going home would be the smart thing to do.

She frowned at the empty room. Her conscience would never allow any such thing. She'd ignored Rachel until it was too late. She'd be a coward to ignore her now.

She owed it to Rachel to find the truth. Rachel had made a mistake by writing her exposé, but people made mistakes every day. If only Kelly had listened. The reality of the situation weighed heavily on Kelly's shoulders. She'd lost her friend forever. But now, she had a chance to clear Rachel's name, to prove her death hadn't been a drug-related accident.

Rachel would have done the same for her.

A few seconds later, Dan reappeared on the top step. "All clear." He closed the space between them, squatting down to rest his strong hands on her knees. He reached up to run a thumb across her jaw. "I'll keep you safe. I promise."

I promise. Kelly brushed a lock of chestnut hair from his forehead, suddenly wanting to stay like this forever. Close to Dan. Sheltered from Miller and the rest of the world.

She squeezed her eyes shut for a moment then met his gaze, the tension between them undeniable. She knew right then she wouldn't leave Summer Shores. Not until they'd seen their investigation through—together.

Dan raised up onto his knees, his face mere inches from hers. Without thinking, Kelly pressed her lips against his, gently at first, then hungrily. She needed the comfort of his touch, needed to lose herself with him, if only for a little while.

Dan's mouth moved to the soft flesh of her neck, his hands slipping to her sides, his thumbs brushing the swells of her breasts.

Apprehension swelled in her gut, but she ignored it. She wanted him. Wanted to feel his skin against hers, his hands on her body again. More than anything, she wanted him inside her, longed to give herself to him completely. Her need was more terrifying than anything she'd ever felt.

Kelly arched her back, letting her body press into his touch. He unbuttoned her blouse then freed the clasp of her bra. She inhaled sharply as he palmed her breasts. When he suckled one pert nipple into his mouth, warmth and want raced through her. His lips and tongue teased and tasted, ratcheting up her need.

Kelly wound her fingers through his hair then cradled his face between her palms, raising his gaze to meet hers. His blue eyes were hooded, full of desire. For her. The sight sent a thrill of awareness straight to the heat pooling between her thighs.

"I need you." Her words were barely a whisper now. "Please."

In one fluid motion, Dan took her hand, pulling her to her feet and slipping his arms around her waist. Her naked flesh brushed against the course weave of his sweater as his mouth closed over hers. His hands slid over her buttocks, pulling her greedily against him. Kelly's breath caught at the feel of his erection pressing against her belly.

"I was a fool to think I could keep my distance." The words sent shock waves of emotion racing through her. She was falling for him and there was no denying that fact. The thought terrified and thrilled her.

Dan hoisted her into his arms, carrying her down the hall to the bed. As he lowered her onto her back, she wondered for a brief moment if she'd forgotten to make the bed. Craziness. Dan was about to make love to her. Who cared about whether or not the bed was made?

He undid the rest of the buttons on her blouse, lowering his lips to her exposed flesh, trailing a hot path to the waistband of her jeans.

Kelly yearned to rip off his clothes and strip from the rest of hers, needing to feel him inside of her, *now.* But the waiting, the teasing, the building toward their joining was ecstasy. A slow, wonderful torture she wished could last forever.

Dan unzipped her jeans, sliding them swiftly down her legs. She wiggled free and he dropped the denim into a heap on the floor. Pressing his lips to her navel, he lowered himself on top of her. A soft moan escaped Kelly's lips.

Dan caressed her body with his mouth in a slow, sensual dance of lips and tongue, nipping at the satin of her panties. She wouldn't last. *Couldn't* last.

"Dan," she whispered. "Please. Now."

He pulled himself to the side of the bed, peeling off his sweater, T-shirt, jeans and boxers.

The moonlight washed through the French doors as she watched, awed by the play of light and shadows on the planes and valleys of his body. So beautiful. So male. So perfect.

The wrapper of the foil crackled, and he sheathed himself. "I had hoped to romance you a bit first." His husky voice only heightened her hunger. "We'll have to make time for that later."

Kelly wrapped her legs around his hips as he lowered himself on top of her, slipping inside effortlessly, her body welcoming, wanting. His strokes filled her, carrying her to a mindless place of shimmering light and release.

As Dan's moans of pleasure came, Kelly matched him, crying out into the darkness of the room with abandon.

Dan cupped her backside, pulling her tight against him as he made one final thrust. A second wave of release blindsided her and she cried out, tears of shock and wonderment welling in her eyes.

Dan relaxed against her, his body covering hers. He trailed one finger across her cheek. "So beautiful."

She wrapped her arms around his neck, lifting to press a kiss to his mouth. "We're a perfect fit."

Dan kneeled between her legs, pulling her into a

hug, his arms supporting her satiated body, holding her to him, crushing her breasts against the warm flesh of his chest.

Kelly's desire reawakened and she moved slowly, rubbing and teasing. He went hard against her belly then pulled her onto his lap. She sat astride him, relishing the feel of him slipping inside, filling her completely.

She moved slowly at first, savoring the sensation as his moves stroked raw nerve endings she hadn't thought capable of additional pleasure. Heat pulsed through her body as Dan suckled her breast, his tongue and teeth teasing one nipple as her body tightened, pulsing against him.

Her orgasm came quickly, crashing through her like a wave against the shore, chased by ripples of aftershock. Dan groaned, pulling her down on top of him. As she settled her head into the hollow of his neck, she squeezed her eyes shut for a moment, wanting to savor this feeling forever.

Her gaze flickered to the desk where the light of the moon caught something. Something she didn't recognize. She struggled to regain her concentration, to pull her dulled senses back to reality. Pushing up for a better view, she cried out. Only this time her cry wasn't one of pleasure, but of fear.

Chapter Nine

Kelly sat at the kitchen table nursing a cup of cold coffee. Helen held her hand, squeezing it tight.

Worry shimmered in her pale blue eyes. "At least you weren't here when he got in."

The police cruiser's strobe lights cast slashes of color through the kitchen blinds. Kelly couldn't help but wonder if Miller was somewhere watching. Laughing.

Her body continued to tremble. Somehow, she couldn't seem to will her muscles to stop the shaking that had started the moment she'd seen the photo propped against the computer.

I came to see you and you weren't here. I don't like that.

She shuddered and Helen tightened her grip on her hand. She shot the woman a weak smile, willing away the cold fear that hung over her like a wall of fog.

Miller had been in her house, in her bedroom. He'd touched her things. He'd photographed her in her sleep. He'd shot at she and Dan in the cemetery. My God, what would he do next?

Dan and Jake argued over procedure while a lone technician worked to lift fingerprints from the French doors. The photo sat on the table, sealed in a plastic bag. A single black-and-white glossy on Agfa paper.

"Don't worry," Jake said as he stepped away from Dan. "We'll get to the bottom of this."

"It's Miller, isn't it?" she asked.

"Of course it's Miller," Dan interrupted, dragging a hand across his forehead and through his hair. Dark stubble dotted his strong jaw, the lines of his face sharp with tension. "I've been trying to tell you this for months, Jake."

"Well, you have my attention." Jake refocused on Kelly. "I hate to say this, but there isn't much we can do at this point. I'll have a car drive by every hour during the night, and we'll keep an eye on Miller." He frowned. "The bottom line is I can't go after him because of this photo."

"You've got to be kidding." Disbelief shone in Dan's glare.

Jake shrugged.

"What about the Oxygesic?"

"What about it? You're talking about two separate things." He tapped the corner of the evidence bag. "This is a nuisance. The other is something for which we have no proof."

"We're building a case." Dan stepped close, his body language taut, strained.

Jake arched a brow. "Really? Like what?"

"Kelly saw a college kid pay cash to fill a prescription at Miller's. We saw the same kid in a bar at Norfolk Community. He thought Kelly wanted to buy from him. He told her he'd already sold out for the night."

Jake stood still, taking a deep breath. Anger flashed in his glare. "You did what?" His voice boomed. He turned to Kelly and she cringed. "Did you accuse him of selling?"

"He brought it up." She straightened, holding her chin high. She had no reason to be intimidated by Jake Arnold. She and Dan had done nothing except search for answers where he'd given them none.

"He accused me of being a reporter," she continued. "Maybe he'd been through this with Rachel." She stood, pointing a finger toward Jake. "Or maybe he'd been warned by Miller to watch out for reporters."

Jake shook his head. A frown tugged at his tired features. "Or maybe you two have gotten carried away with your witch hunt."

Kelly sank back into the chair, lowering her face to her palms, too weary to continue the argument. Helen gently rubbed her back.

"You need to knock it off." Jake's tone left no doubt he meant business.

Dan pulled out the chair next to Kelly, eyeing her intently. "Jake's right. Let's not get Miller any more fired up than he already is."

Yet the look that passed between them spoke volumes. Both knew they were nowhere near being done with Vince Miller.

DAN LEFT shortly after Helen and the police cleared out. A lone patrol car sat on the street, standing vigil.

Kelly felt protected. Safe. For now. Her trembling had stopped, but a deep chill persisted in her bones.

She stacked the last of the coffee cups in the sink and turned for the bedroom. Dark powder smudged the frame of the French doors. The technician said he'd found nothing. Miller must have been wearing gloves or he'd rubbed down any surfaces he'd touched.

She pulled a tissue from the box next to her bed and wiped at the door frame. Frowning at her lack of progress, she tossed the tissue at the trashcan under Rachel's desk. It fell short.

"Rats."

She dropped to her knees and reached. A second object glimmered, and she hooked it with her fingertips. A candy wrapper. She backed out from beneath the desk to sit on her haunches.

Jolly Roger. Grape. She shook her head.

You'd think people would be more careful.

HE STEPPED quickly across the gravel, stopping at the store's back entrance. Effortlessly, he slipped a key into the lock and pulled the door open. A shrill whistle filled the air as he punched in the alarm code. Silence. Good. The number hadn't been changed.

The cluttered room smelled heavily of must, as usual. He stepped over a pile of boxes then pulled the door shut behind him. He twisted his pocket flashlight, casting a narrow beam of light through the tight space. The pictures had to be here somewhere. Somewhere in this mess.

He lifted and sifted through piles, not worried

about prints. The latex gloves would take care of that. Working his way from one corner of the room to another, he found only inventory files, crossword puzzles and *Penthouse* magazines. Miller had one heck of a gig here. Regular model citizen.

Just as he was growing annoyed, the glossy edge of a black-and-white print peeked from beneath a stack of folders. He pulled it free, smiling. A portrait of a woman. Perfect.

He slipped the manila envelope from his backpack and untied the flap. He pulled out shot after shot of Kelly. At her computer. On her deck. In her bed. He replaced Miller's print, slipped the new images beneath and laughed.

His mouth felt dry as he stepped back out into the damp Outer Banks air. He pulled a hard candy from his pocket and peeled off the wrapper. Root beer. His favorite. Sweets for the sweet.

He laughed again as he headed for his car. If only everything could be this easy.

THE NEXT MORNING, Kelly spread Vince's photographs across the bed, turning each over one by one. Fuji paper. Every single shot he'd given her for the brochure had been printed on Fuji paper. No Agfa.

She'd mocked up the brochure shortly after he'd given her the prints, and had thought she'd remembered the paper differently from what had been left last night.

She rubbed her chin and frowned. It didn't mean a whole lot, she guessed. The guy could certainly use more than one type of paper to develop his shots. But the discrepancy nagged at her.

What if Miller hadn't left the photo? Or what if he was only part of a larger group? What if she was the target of someone she and Dan hadn't stopped to consider? Someone other than Miller.

Kelly shoved the thought from her mind and gathered the photos, returning them to their case. Of course Miller had left her the photo. He was trying to scare her off, and Kelly Weir didn't scare off. Not when her friend was dead, and possibly murdered. She hadn't felt passionate about much of anything for the past year, but the questions swirling behind Rachel's drowning had reignited a fire in Kelly's belly she'd thought long dead.

Dan's deep blue eyes and strong features flashed across her mind. Even if he walked away from her when this was all over, she'd learned from him. His intensity and strength of conviction had brought her back to life.

She was engrossed in her thoughts when the phone rang.

"Dan?"

Silence grew at the other end of the line. Her pulse quickened.

"Anyone there?"

"Were you expecting Dan?"

Miller's voice sent ice screaming through her veins.

"Ah," she stammered. "Yes…he was going to help me with…something."

"I'll bet." Disdain tinged Miller's mutter.

Kelly fought to keep her voice calm. She refused to let him sense the fear slicing through her. "I was just looking at your brochure design. It's funny you should call."

"I was out for a drive. Thought I'd stop by to see how you are. You hungry? We could go grab some breakfast."

"Maybe another time." Cold apprehension seeped through her tired bones. "I need to work on packing Rachel's things."

"Convenient." Disgust filled his voice.

She was wondering how to soothe his anger when gravel crunched in the driveway. Her stomach pitched. It couldn't be—

"I won't stay but a minute." Vince lowered his voice, his words whispering across the line. "I'd love to see what you've done with my photos."

The phone went dead in Kelly's ear. She dialed Dan's number with shaking fingers. He answered on the second ring.

"Miller's here." The words tumbled from her lips. "Hurry."

She disconnected without waiting for an answer.

THE SHARP GRAVEL of the drive cut into the soles of Dan's bare feet, sending daggers of pain up his calves. There was no time to go back for shoes. He cranked the Karmann Ghia's ignition and jammed the gearshift into first.

How could Miller be at her house? Damn it. Dan should have stayed with her, ignoring Jake's directive to go home and leave protecting Kelly to the police.

Pressing the accelerator to the floor, he pulled out

onto Shore Road without looking. There wasn't time to look. There wasn't time for anything but getting to Kelly.

Waves of fear washed through him. He shouldn't have left her alone. If Miller touched one hair, he'd kill him with his bare hands.

Dan shuddered, not willing to imagine Kelly getting hurt or worse. She'd gotten under his skin, affecting him as no woman ever had.

Shoving his emotions to the back of his brain, he swung the car onto Kelly's street, skidding to a stop in the drive. Gravel flew into the side of Miller's van where it sat next to Kelly's Jetta.

Panic seized Dan's heart as he leaped from the car, taking the wooden stairs two at a time.

KELLY HANDED Vince the folder of photos and he smiled. "Well? Did you like them?"

"They're gorgeous," she said. "I notice you use only Fuji paper."

Vince stroked a slender finger across one of his prints. "It gives the black and white a hint of blue." He raised his cold gaze to meet hers. She tamped down the shudder threatening to crawl across her shoulders. "It's the only paper I ever use."

She nodded, doing her best to look calm. He spoke the words convincingly, though he could be a smooth liar. Who was she kidding? Of course the man was a smooth liar.

"Here." She pulled the brochure sample from a folder on the desk. "I hope you like it."

He studied the design closely, opening the trifold

to read every word, his gaze caressing every shot. A wide grin spread across his face as he looked up at her. His smile sent her insides tilting sideways. She longed to turn and run for her life, but she held her ground.

"You're quite talented." Miller nodded at the brochure.

Kelly faked a smile, hoping she looked sincere. "No, you're the one with talent. How long have you been into photography?"

He arched a brow, rubbing his chin. "Long as I can remember."

"Where's your darkroom?"

"Back at my house. I converted a bathroom."

"Can I ask you a question about your technique?" Her pulse quickened, her heart pounding in her ears.

Vince brightened.

"The profile of the one woman. How did you get her to look so natural? I'd almost think she didn't know she was being photographed."

"She didn't." Vince straightened, smirking. "Telephoto lens. She never knew I was anywhere around."

And neither had Kelly. Yet she'd seen proof of his technique left in this very house.

Footsteps slammed on the front steps. Dan appeared barefoot in the doorway, his blue eyes dark and wild, bright color flushing his cheeks.

Kelly's stomach somersaulted at the intensity of emotion etched across his face.

Vince's eyes grew wide. "What's the matter, Steele? Afraid I might steal this girlfriend, too?"

"Hardly."

Dan closed the space between them, twisting his fingers into the fabric of Miller's shirt. He shoved him against the wall. Kelly gasped at the ferocity of the move.

"Had a break-in last night, Vince. You wouldn't know anything about that, would you?"

Miller pulled Dan's fingers from his collar, smoothing the front of his shirt. He narrowed his eyes, pressing his lips into a tight, flat line. "I don't know what you're talking about, but I don't like the implication."

"Stay away from Kelly. Understood?"

Kelly felt Dan's rage from where she stood. His fury frightened and thrilled her at the same time. Like a wild man crazed with possessiveness, he shoved Miller against the wall again.

"Dan," she whispered.

"Stay away from her," Dan repeated his warning.

"Did she tell you she's doing work for me? Maybe you should get your facts straight before you go off half-cocked."

Dan released him and stepped away, pacing wildly.

Miller turned to Kelly. "I'm sorry for the interruption. I'll leave you to get your friend settled down." He gave Dan another long look. "If you *can* get him settled down." He leveled a cool gaze at Kelly. She fought the urge to wrap her arms around herself. "The brochure is lovely. If you could run a few copies and give me a disk, I'll get the rest printed professionally."

She nodded, doing her best to ignore the shocked look Dan threw her.

"You're going to finish his brochure?"

His rage startled her. "It's already done." She lightly touched his arm. "It's done."

"I'll be in touch," Miller said over his shoulder as he left. He stopped in the doorway, turning back. "Kelly. When you get tired of Mr. Steele's possessive nature, you know where to find me. Rachel did."

Dan's arm tensed beneath Kelly's fingertips. She tightened her grasp. She held on until gravel crunched loudly as Miller's van pulled out of the drive.

Dan sank onto the bed and ran his hands across his face. "I thought he might hurt you—or worse." He looked up at her, his eyes bright with emotion. "You can't imagine the things I thought on the way over here."

Warmth tangled with the nerves dancing in Kelly's stomach. There was no mistaking the genuine concern in Dan's expression.

She kneeled in front of him, splaying her fingers across his knees. "I've never been so frightened in my life. All I could think to do was to call you."

His vivid gaze softened, and awareness sparked between them. He leaned forward, hungrily pressing his lips to hers. Kelly deepened the kiss, longing to forget what had just transpired, but suddenly remembered Miller's parting shot. She pulled back.

"What did he mean about Rachel?"

Dan hesitated visibly, his gaze widening.

And to think she'd begun to let this man into her heart. "You slept with her, too, didn't you?"

Anger flashed in Kelly's brown gaze. "Is this part of *your* pattern? Do you involve all your investigative assistants emotionally? Make them care? Get them to cooperate?" She squeezed her eyes shut and drew in a deep breath. "I believed you. Fell for you."

"Kelly, please." Damn, he couldn't believe this.

He reached for her, but she turned away. He should have told her when he first met her, or at least once he'd suspected she harbored old wounds. He'd seen the glimmer of distrust in her eyes, like a puppy that had been kicked one time too many.

Kelly straightened, pointing toward the hallway. "Please leave."

"Be reasonable. That's all in the past. Rachel and I were only friends." But, Kelly…Kelly had come to mean…everything.

"Now." The word rang out like an open-handed slap.

Dan positioned himself in front of the bedroom door, turning her to face him. Unshed tears glistened in her dark eyes. His heart twisted.

"Go."

He flinched at the sharp edge of her tone. "I should have told you, but I was afraid this would happen."

"What?" Incredulity distorted her features. "You were afraid I'd be upset? Or you were afraid I wouldn't help you find your answers?"

Kelly looked away, but he cupped her chin gently, coaxing her gaze to his. "What's going on between us is real, Kelly."

Her breath caught and a lone tear tumbled down her cheek. "I don't believe you."

"I'm not sure what happened between you and this Brian you mentioned." He brushed his lips across her forehead, steeling himself against the hurt when she pulled away. "All I know is I'm not some ex-lover, and you're sure as hell not Rachel."

He released her shoulders and stepped into the hall, stopping at the front door. "Think about what I said, because I've never been more sure of anything in my life."

KELLY SANK to the floor, leaned against the bed and let the tears fall. Tears for Rachel. Tears for her own stupidity. Tears for the pain that tore at her heart.

How dare he talk about real?

His words haunted her. She pulled a pillow from the bed and hugged it, burying her face and crying until moisture soaked the cotton fabric.

She'd let herself fall for him, believing he cared about her, not about her ability to help him expose Miller or whoever was behind the illegal Oxygesic. But he was no different than Brian had been. Dan had used her. Plain and simple. He'd manipulated Rachel's investigative skills before her death and now he'd swung his attentions over to Kelly.

Her heart twisted in protest to her thoughts. Fresh tears welled in her eyes at the thought of his reaction at the cemetery and today with Miller. Had he been faking? How could you fake such raw emotion?

A noise sounded next to her and something soft brushed past. She looked up from the pillow into Edgar's wide, yellow eyes. The cat's broad head tipped to one side then he touched a paw to her knee. She scooped him into her lap.

A shadow darkened the bedroom door. Helen stood in the threshold, a bowl of tomatoes cradled in the bend of her arm. "Thought you might like these."

Kelly choked back a sob and nodded.

Helen set the bowl on the desk, lowered herself to the floor and wrapped one arm around Kelly's shoulder. Kelly gladly softened into Helen's warm embrace, feeling like she'd known the kind-hearted, no-nonsense woman all her life.

Helen's kind tone soothed her. "Still upset about the photo?"

Kelly told Helen what had happened and explained Dan's forced admission regarding his affair with Rachel.

Helen arched her brows. She shrugged, twisting her mouth sideways. "So Steele didn't come clean of his own free will. At least he admitted it once you asked."

"But with Rachel," Kelly whispered.

"Don't confuse his past with your present." The elderly woman stood, fisting her hands on her hips. "It only takes one look at the two of you to know how you feel about each other."

Kelly raised her chin to meet Helen's gaze. "What if he's only using me to go after Miller?"

Helen shook her head. "Some things you can't fake, sweetie. Trust me on this. I'm old. I know things you don't."

Kelly smiled in spite of herself, wiping away the last trace of her tears with a dry corner of the pillow.

"Don't let pride destroy your chance at happiness," Helen said.

"Like it did my friendship with Rachel." The familiar regret swept through her.

Helen patted Kelly's head. "And now you're trying to redeem yourself. And you will." She snapped her fingers. Edgar sauntered instantly to her side.

Kelly pulled herself to her feet. "Thanks."

Helen took a step toward the hallway, the bowl in the crook of her arm. "I'll leave these in the kitchen for you." She turned back at the bedroom door. "I think you know what you need to do."

DAN SAT on the deck, brushing the dirt and sand from his bare, bloodied feet. The damp September air hung heavy with salt. The ocean roared, its steel-gray waves slapping against the deserted shoreline.

He leaned back against the slats of the chair and shut his eyes. For the first time ever, someone mattered more than Diane. More than his mother. More than himself. *Kelly.*

He let out a frustrated sigh. He ached with fatigue, his bones heavy from months of wondering if he'd caused his sister's death. If he'd contributed to his mother's decline.

Now he could add Rachel's death to the list.

A sliver of pain slipped through the protective wall he'd erected around his heart. He hadn't allowed himself much of a reaction to Rachel's death except anger. But now the sadness came, mingling with the guilt he carried deep inside.

Yet here he sat, on the deck of his oceanfront

home bought with stock profits earned for the marketing of Oxygesic. He shook his head, ashamed of himself.

He was glad Kelly finally knew about Rachel, though the physical part of their relationship had been nothing more than a one-night stand. He had wanted Rachel only for the information she might find on Miller. Their partnership had grown into friendship. His liaison with Kelly had grown into far more. His stomach tightened, twisting into an anxious, coiled knot.

If he hadn't already lost Kelly for good, he'd surely lose her once she discovered the whole truth behind his frantic investigation into the deaths of Diane and Rachel.

Would she understand why he needed to ease his mind? Why he needed to know he wasn't somehow responsible? After all, he'd helped push the drug through an expedited FDA approval, developed the marketing plan, the collateral materials, the pitch, the pricing. You name it.

Now the drug meant to be a breakthrough for those with chronic pain had become a curse to those with a weakness for a quick high.

Dan's thoughts lingered on the sensation of Kelly's ample curves pressed against his bare skin and the pure abandon of losing himself inside her. He ran a hand through his hair and stood.

He couldn't do this to himself. There was no time to wallow. No time to reminisce. He had to go forward. Had to keep moving.

This time tomorrow he'd have answers from Scott

Jansen. Maybe, just maybe, he'd finally have enough to make Jake believe his theories on Miller.

Beyond that, he had to figure out a way to keep Kelly safe. She might want nothing to do with him, but he had no intention of leaving her vulnerable to Miller. Perhaps she was so angry she'd return home, leaving Summer Shores and danger behind.

Dan rubbed a hand across his tired face, the grim reality of the situation settling into his bones. Kelly might not be a reporter, but she had tenacity like he'd never seen. She'd never leave without discovering the truth. That meant she'd become a sitting duck—for Miller and his madness.

He walked gingerly across the wooden planks of the deck, breathing a sigh of relief when his battered feet touched the cool tile of the living room.

He tried Kelly's number, but the phone rang without answer. He plucked a beer from the refrigerator then headed toward the den. Time to jot down a list of questions for Jansen. He couldn't afford to forget anything when they met. Plus, focusing on the meeting would help take his mind off of how he'd left things with Kelly.

The door to his office sat partially closed. He frowned, trying to remember if he'd left it that way. When he stepped into the paneled room, the disarray registered before he had a chance to feel trepidation.

His desk had been ransacked, his file drawers dumped on the floor. Papers lay strewn, tossed and shredded from one side of the room to the other.

A shuffling noise startled him and he ducked,

spinning as he raised the beer bottle. Too late. A blinding flash of pain ripped through his head and neck. Then another.

Dan's body failed him as his world turned to black.

Chapter Ten

Kelly stood at Dan's front door and drew in a long, slow breath. She could do this. She could let herself trust him enough to forgive his not telling her about Rachel. He was only human, after all. Even more important, she'd chosen to believe he cared about her, not just about her ability to help him with the investigation.

It was time to let go of the specter of Brian.

She wouldn't be foolish, however. Surely the passion she and Dan shared was at least partially due to the danger of their circumstances.

What's going on between us is real, Kelly.

Dan's words echoed within her, teasing her to believe. Her doubt persisted, niggling at the base of her skull like a throbbing reminder of her desire for self-preservation.

Vowing not to let smoke and mirrors break her heart, Kelly rang the doorbell and waited. Nothing.

She leaned on the bell once more, knocking. Again, nothing. Peeking through the narrow windows on either side of the door, she frowned, spotting no movement whatsoever. Odd. Dan's car sat in the driveway. Maybe he was out back on the deck.

She made her way through the soft sand and climbed the deck stairs. An empty chair sat close to the railing, facing the roaring ocean. Dan was nowhere in sight.

Kelly pressed her forehead against the slider to peer into the living room and kitchen. The afternoon had grown dark, yet no lamps glowed inside.

She tapped on the glass door, counting to ten before she tried the handle. Unlocked. She slid the door open and stepped inside.

"Dan? You here? Dan?"

She stopped short, waiting for his response. Nothing. Her heart raced. A shiver danced up her spine and her skin erupted in goose bumps. She chided herself for watching too many scary movies in her life.

"I came to talk to you." Her voice disappeared into the silent void of the house.

Kelly moved slowly toward the hall. Maybe he'd gone for a walk on the beach to clear his head. That would be a logical answer. After all, he did live along one of the most beautiful stretches of beach around.

Soft light spilled into the hall from one of the doors, and she headed straight for it. Her breath caught as she cleared the door frame. The room had been ransacked. Dan lay facedown in a pile of papers.

Kelly dropped to her knees and checked his wrist for a pulse. Good and strong. *Thank God.* Tears welled in her eyes, but she blinked them back. Now was not the time for emotion.

She lowered her lips to his ear. "Dan. Can you

hear me?" Her heart beat so loudly the sound alone might be enough to wake him. She wanted to assess his injuries, but didn't dare move him. She needed help fast.

Kelly scrambled for the phone, lifting the receiver just as Dan moaned.

"Don't call anyone," he murmured.

She dropped the phone and rushed to his side. "Dan."

"Don't call." His pain was palpable in his words.

Was he crazy? He could be seriously injured. "I'm calling an ambulance. And the police. What happened?"

"Hit me." His voice had become weak and thready. "In my office."

Kelly's heart slammed into her throat. What if someone was still in the house?

"We need to call the police." She looked down at his pale face, and her heart caught. What if she hadn't come over? What if the intruder had done more than knock him out? What if—?

Dan rolled to one side, his eyelids fluttering open. "Sure he's gone by now." He closed his eyes. "Don't call…"

His voice trailed away, and Kelly feared he'd slipped into unconsciousness again. She slid her hand beneath his head and stroked his cheek. "Can you hear me?"

His eyes winked open.

Sheer relief washed through her.

Dan pulled himself onto an elbow in an effort to sit up. He held his head and swore.

"Did you see who hit you?"

"No, but I'm sure it was Miller."

She shuddered. Was this Miller's payback for Dan's earlier outburst? "How can you be sure?"

"Because I really pissed him off today. It makes sense." Dan rolled his neck and grimaced. "He probably came straight here and rifled my office. Braining me over the head was an added treat."

"I'm calling Jake."

Dan shook his head then winced. "No. Not this time." He leveled his gaze at Kelly, intensity burning in his eyes. "We're getting close. We need to keep pushing."

"You could have been killed." Just saying the words made her feel sick inside. She couldn't imagine what she'd do if anything worse had happened to him. Then it hit her. Dan had been right.

What they shared went far deeper than this case.

"But I wasn't." The pain in his voice snapped her attention back to his injuries.

Kelly touched the side of his head. A knot the size of a jumbo egg had swollen beneath the spot where her fingers gingerly touched his scalp.

"At least let me take you to the hospital."

"No way." His brows pulled into a deep furrow. "It's just you and me now." His gaze flicked up to her face. "If you're still in this with me."

She stared at him for a long moment then let out a sigh. "I'm with you."

"WE NEED TO get back inside his store," Dan said.

Kelly held his head in her lap. A glass of scotch sat between them and a roaring fire. The weather had turned and sheets of rain pelted the sliding glass doors.

Dan repositioned the ice pack with a frown. "I'll go."

Kelly laughed. "Like Miller's going to let you within a mile of his back room."

Dan arched a brow. "You've got a point."

"I'll run some brochures and take them over. He said he's closing up tonight. I can do it now."

"I'm driving you."

Kelly shook her head. "I don't think you're driving anybody anywhere. You've got a goose egg on your head."

Dan pressed his lips into a tight line. "I'm fine. Little headache, that's all. It's going to take more than a crack on the head to keep me down."

Kelly stroked Dan's hair, her emotions battling within her—warmth, concern, fear, attraction. "Let's not give him the chance, okay?"

"I don't want you there alone with him."

"His staff will be there."

Silence beat between them.

Dan's features tensed. "I'll wait outside. Just in case he pulls something."

"Fine." Kelly straightened. "But I won't let him pull anything. We're going to nail him for what he's done. For all the lives he's destroyed. I wish you'd let me call Jake."

"Jake doesn't want to hear it." Dan squeezed his eyes shut, giving his head a quick shake. "I'm like the boy who cried wolf. I've beat this theory to death and now that we're actually getting somewhere, he doesn't believe me."

"He doesn't want to believe you."

Dan traced a finger down the length of her cheek, radiating warmth through her. "And what about us? Can you forgive me for not telling you about Rachel?"

She nodded slowly. "I'm dealing with it."

"She and I were together once and it meant…" His expression softened, as if he wanted to say more, but wasn't quite ready to let go. "She was only a friend."

The fire reflected orange against Dan's eyes. Genuine emotion swirled in his gaze, and Kelly's resolve to take their relationship carefully started to crumble.

He leaned close, brushing his lips softly against hers. She returned the kiss lightly then pulled away, her emotions warring inside her.

Dan cupped her chin, his expression growing serious. The contact sent desire spiraling to her core. "You have a light within you like I've never seen."

Heat ignited in Kelly's cheeks. She could only hope Dan might think her healthy glow the result of the fire's proximity, not his words. Stunned by his uncharacteristic display of emotion, she stood, carrying his glass of scotch to the kitchen.

She stopped at the sink, gazing out at the surf pounding the shore. Angry storm clouds had rolled in and the current swirled and twisted, leaving a foamy froth in its wake.

The now familiar sensation of dread crawled across Kelly's shoulders. She'd gotten herself in so deep with Dan and with his investigation, she wasn't sure her heart would survive. Hell, she wasn't sure she'd survive.

She shot a glance back to where Dan sat, eyes closed, holding his head. The man didn't know the meaning of the word *quit*. If he believed they were close to the truth—close to finding their answers—then Kelly would trust him.

A shiver ripped through her. Her very survival might depend on this man.

KELLY FOLLOWED Dan within one block of Miller's store. Rain slapped the windshield and wind buffeted the car. The brake lights on Dan's car glowed as he pulled to the side of the road. She pulled alongside and gave him the thumbs-up. Not that he'd be able to see her through the murky night.

She slipped the car into an open parking space then dashed for the apothecary's front door. The store sat empty except for Sarah checking inventory toward the back. No wonder. The posted closing time had passed.

Kelly stopped next to her. "Is Vince in? I thought I'd drop off his brochures."

Sarah looked up, smiling with recognition. "He just ran out to make a delivery. Want to wait for him in the back?"

"Okay." Kelly's pulse pounded in her ears, the lump in her throat threatening to choke her. "Can I ask you a question?"

"Sure."

"Do you guys handle a lot of prescriptions for the institute?"

Sarah nodded, her eyes growing wide. "Thank goodness. If not for them we'd probably have no business. Three of the big chains have stores within a mile of us." She shook her head and frowned. "Poor Vince hasn't done too well since he bought this store."

"I didn't realize." Kelly did her best to look interested, but not too interested.

Sarah lowered her head to focus on her work. "Lucky for Vince he's got a lot of regular customers who don't have prescription coverage. His cash sales are what save him."

Jackpot.

Kelly stepped into the back room, wrinkling her nose at the smell of stale air. She stood still for a moment, letting her eyes adjust to the dark, crowded space. Piles of paperwork, newspapers and boxes covered every inch.

She searched for a clear surface to put down Vince's brochures, but finally gave up, deciding to peek under files and papers. His other photos had to be somewhere in this mess. He'd told her as much himself.

Of course, she'd love to find something about Oxygesic sales, but she didn't think him that careless.

Kelly's elbow hit a stack of files and they slid like a small avalanche toward the edge of the counter. She blocked them with her waist, pushing them back into place. As she did so, a black-and-white image of an arm appeared partway down the stack. She took off the papers above it, exposing the photo, which was identical to the shot left in her bedroom.

Kelly pulled up the corner far enough to see the paper's stamp. Agfa.

"Son of a—"

"You're out late." Vince's voice sounded close. Too close.

Kelly bit back a gasp, shoving the photo into the pile and spinning to face him.

"Sorry, didn't mean to scare you." His cold eyes measured her head to toe. "Sarah said you brought the brochures."

"I did," she answered quickly. Probably too quickly. "I wanted to get them over to you and also tell you how sorry I am about earlier today." *My God, had he seen what she'd found?* She thrust the handful of brochures at him then fumbled in her backpack. "I also brought you a disk with the file on it."

Vince took the brochures, stepping closer. "Feeling okay? You look like a deer caught in the headlights." He chuckled, the sinister sound sending a tremor through her. "I do have that effect on women."

Kelly made the effort to laugh even as icy fear crawled up her neck, sinking into her scalp.

He turned his attention to the brochures. "What do I owe you?"

"I'll send you an invoice. I completely forgot to bring one with me." Breathing had become more difficult, and she moved to pass him, trying to escape the cramped space.

Vince grasped her upper arm and squeezed to the point of discomfort. She refused to squirm, standing still and strong.

"I don't scare you, do I?" His smile grew bright

and wide, but his eyes had gone vacant, devoid of emotion. "I hope Steele didn't fill your head with nonsense about me."

The room pitched sideways. Kelly pulled her arm free of Miller's fingers, stepping toward the door. She laughed, longing to scream for help. She tipped her head coyly. "Why would you scare me?"

"Why don't I take you to dinner as a thank-you for these?"

"Thanks, but I have plans."

"With Steele?" Vince eyed her accusingly.

Kelly nodded.

Miller instantly scowled. "I didn't like how he treated me, did you?"

She shook her head, and he closed the space between them, tucking a strand of hair behind her ear then tracing the line of her jaw with his fingertip. She focused on maintaining a calm expression and steady breathing.

"Sometimes I wonder how far I'll have to go to get your attention." Vince's voice had grown robotic, kicking Kelly's internal alarm to full panic.

"You have my attention, but I have to leave."

She turned and rushed for the exit door, half expecting his fingers to close around her arm, her shoulder, her neck. Was this how Rachel had felt? Terrified? Trapped?

When the pouring rain hit her face, she realized she wasn't breathing. She inhaled deeply and leaned against her car as she jammed the key in the lock.

"Kelly, wait," Vince called out from the open door. "I want to pay you."

"We'll worry about that later." She climbed into the driver's seat, slamming the door shut and slapping on the lock.

As she passed Dan's car, she flashed her brights, watching her rearview mirror until the Karmann Ghia's brake lights illuminated. She pulled to the shoulder and waited. By the time he parked behind her and rapped on her window, tears tumbled uncontrollably down her cheeks.

She pressed the unlock button, and Dan yanked open her door. He swept her into his arms, and she gratefully stood in the pouring rain, her face buried against his chest.

"What happened?" Dan's tone was frantic. "Did he touch you? Did he hurt you?"

She shook her head against his chest, unable to do anything more than cling to him.

"Come on, there's a little place down the way. Follow me. Let's get you out of this rain and away from here."

THEY SLID into opposite sides of the booth and Dan ordered two coffees. Kelly looked calmer now, though her eyes remained wide and frightened. He'd kill Miller with his bare hands if given the chance.

"I found something." Kelly sounded exhausted, her voice cracking. She straightened, as if trying to hide how scared she'd been.

"What?" Dan stared intently, searching her face.

"I found the same picture buried under a pile of files."

"Just one?" His pulsed quickened and he leaned toward her.

"There might have been more, but that's when Vince walked in."

He squeezed his eyes shut and groaned. "Did he see what you were doing?"

"I don't know."

"How was he acting?"

"More threatening than usual." She blew out a breath. "Definitely trying to intimidate me."

"Start at the beginning. Tell me exactly what happened and what he said."

Kelly explained what she'd seen, and all that she and Vince had said to each other.

"What do you think?" she asked when she finished.

He exhaled to relieve the tension squeezing his chest. "This has gone too far." He slapped a palm on the tabletop. "I can't involve you in this anymore."

She shook her head, her expression growing defiant. "No way. Don't shut me out of this now. I'm going with you tomorrow to the pharmacy board."

Dan took a long sip of his coffee, watching her wordlessly.

"What?" Her eyes narrowed.

"I changed my mind. I'm going to Jake one more time."

Kelly frowned. "I thought you wanted to do this without him?"

"I can't risk your safety."

The color drained from her cheeks. "You think Vince will come after me?"

He started to answer honestly, but caught himself, not wanting to scare her any more than she'd already been scared tonight. "Just wait for me at Helen's while I go to Jake's."

She shook her head. "I'll go with you."

"I'll get further without you."

He watched the emotions flicker across her beautiful face, knowing she was remembering how tight-lipped Jake became whenever she was near.

"Okay." She nodded. "But you've got to call me as soon as you leave his office."

"Deal."

DAN STEPPED to the door of Jake's office and stopped. Jake was in the middle of a rant.

"Well, the thing is," Jake growled into the phone, "If you weren't such a loose cannon, this wouldn't be an issue." His back faced the door, his feet sat propped on the steel credenza.

Dan tapped on the door frame. Jake looked over his shoulder and raised a finger. "Listen, I gotta go," he said into the receiver. "Don't call me until you figure this out."

He hung up the phone then turned to wave Dan in. "Danny boy. What can I do for you now?"

Dan nodded toward the phone. "Sounded like a pleasant conversation."

"Ah, they all are." Jake shrugged. "Some career I picked."

Dan decided to cut the chitchat. "Kelly went to see Miller."

Jake stopped short then rubbed a hand across his

face. "I asked her specifically to stay away from him."

Dan had no time to listen to Jake. Kelly had seen the proof they needed. "She saw a picture."

"Of what?"

"Same picture we found in her room yesterday."

"She sure?" Jake's pale eyes widened.

"Miller walked in on her, but she's pretty sure. She thought there might be others, but she didn't get time to look."

"Did Miller see what she'd found?"

"I don't think so."

"What did he say to her?" Jake flipped open a notebook and started writing.

"He was more threatening than usual. She's genuinely scared." Impatience simmered in Dan's gut. "Can we move on this now?"

Jake leaned across his desk. "I'll have a talk with him."

"He had to be in her house to leave that photo."

"There were no prints. Look, maybe I can get him to come clean."

"Maybe?" Dan flattened his palm against the desk, fighting the urge to throttle his friend. "You're telling me you can't check out the back room at his store?" He stood and paced the small office. "She saw the same photo. What more do you need?"

"Probable cause for the search warrant. That's what."

Hot anger fired in Dan's cheeks. "Jake. She's a sitting duck."

"I'll have a car patrol her street through the night. She'll be fine." Jake shrugged. "What could possibly go wrong?"

Chapter Eleven

Kelly's silhouette appeared at the porch door as Dan pulled his car into her drive. His body hummed to life at the sight of her. He realized all of his determination to keep the wall around his heart had failed. It took only one glimpse to know he was a goner.

He'd called after leaving Jake's office to tell her a patrol car would be by through the night, explaining he'd fill her in on the rest when he reached her house.

"Well?" Her voice cut through the damp, salt air as he neared the top of the steps.

"Wasted trip." Dan grimaced, briefly squeezing his eyes shut. "He'll talk to Miller, that's all."

She gave him a weak smile and helped him out of his soaking wet jacket. "At least he's willing to do that."

"You're right."

Kelly pressed her fingertips to his cheek, and he leaned into the warmth of her touch, wanting to forget Miller. Just for a moment he wanted to forget that his sister and Rachel were dead. He wanted to steal a moment to lose himself in Kelly's embrace, to pretend her life wasn't in danger.

Her brown eyes widened. "How's your head?"

He nodded. "I'll survive."

Concern shone in the depths of her dark gaze. He hadn't thought it possible to care for her so deeply. She'd broken through the wall around his heart and settled there, like a favorite old quilt, comfortable and warm. And, although she hadn't said as much, he knew she felt the same.

Despite their deepening bond, Dan couldn't let himself want her. Not now. The attacks were escalating. If he lost his focus, Miller could win. For Dan, that wasn't an option.

The rumble of an engine caught his attention, and he turned toward the street. The patrol car.

Dan took a step backward on the porch, away from the temptation of Kelly. "I'll pick you up a little after seven tomorrow. We don't want to be late meeting Jansen."

Confusion washed across her face. "You aren't coming in?"

He shook his head, his heart squeezing in protest. "Not tonight."

Kelly nodded, her brows furrowed. "You should be resting anyway. I wish you'd let me take you to a doctor."

He rubbed the lump on his head and winced. "This is nothing."

She closed the space between them and pressed her hand to his head, checking his scalp. Her gaze shifted from her touch to his eyes. Heat spiked between them, and her tongue skimmed across her lower lip, leaving a moist trail in its path.

Dan swallowed, all thoughts of objectivity scattering from his brain. He closed his mouth over hers, drinking deeply of her sweetness. Kelly's fingers wound through his hair, stroking the back of his neck.

He battled against the carnal need throbbing inside him. He couldn't stay with her. Not tonight. She'd be safe, protected by the patrol officer outside. Tonight, Dan needed distance from the emotions Kelly had sparked to life.

He captured her hands and broke their embrace, pushing her away. She stiffened, her lips parting in surprise.

"We can't do this now. It's too dangerous."

Dan dropped her hands, racing down the steps before Kelly could utter a word. Her shocked expression burned into his mind as he drove home.

Leaving her now was for the best. He had to regain the objectivity and control he'd lost if he wanted to outsmart Miller. And this time, he would.

THE TAPPING on the French door startled Kelly from sleep the next morning. She glanced bleary-eyed at the alarm clock. Six o'clock. Her stomach flip-flopped as she struggled to acclimate herself.

"Who's there?"

"It's Jake Arnold. I need to talk to you."

She rubbed the sleep from her eyes, climbing from bed to pull a sweatshirt over her head before she opened the door.

"What's going on?" Her heart thumped rapid beats against her ribs. "Is everything all right?"

Jake nodded, his expression serious. "Can I come in?"

"Sure. I'll make some coffee."

"I brought you some. Figured I could at least do that much since I was waking you up at the crack of dawn."

"Why didn't you use the front?" She gestured toward the door as they walked down the hall.

"I thought you might not be able to hear me."

Kelly led him into the kitchen. Jake hoisted two foam coffee cups out of a white paper bag and set one in front of her. She flipped off the lid to take a quick sip. He plucked a glazed donut from a second bag and slid it across the table.

"What's going on?" Confusion whirled through her. Why was he here? Now? To tell her what?

"You need to know some things about Dan."

"Dan?" Her empty stomach rolled and she pushed the donut away. "Is he okay?"

Jake nodded. "He's fine. But you deserve all of the facts before you continue the witch hunt he's got you on."

Anger warmed Kelly's cheeks. "It's not a witch hunt. I don't understand why you won't step in with the evidence we've got."

"I plan to speak with Miller, but you need to understand something." He shook his head, a crease forming between his brows. "Dan's made it his personal mission to take Miller down. You need to know why."

She straightened and leaned forward. "I know why. He thinks Miller killed his sister."

Jake shook his head, his expression softening. "Oxygesic killed his sister, and Dan helped develop Oxygesic."

The room spun. Kelly splayed her fingers on the tabletop to keep herself upright. Surely she hadn't heard correctly. "He developed Oxygesic?"

"Helped develop." Jake didn't speak for several seconds, as if he were letting her recover from the shock of what he'd said. "Dan was a company executive, in charge of marketing and sales. Where do you think his stock riches came from?"

She shook her head, stunned.

"Stock options. He made his fortune off of Oxygesic before he left the company. Before people started to abuse the drug and die."

"But surely that can't be his fault."

"In his eyes, it is." Jake stood and pushed his chair under the table. "Oxygesic played a role in his sister's death. Think about it."

"Why are you telling me this?" She stood to meet his gaze head-on. "I thought you were his friend."

"I am. And I've been trying to get him to move on with his life for a long time." He paused, glancing down at the table before leveling a look that shook Kelly to the core. "He's using you to help clear his conscience, just like he used Rachel."

"And she ended up dead," Kelly said flatly.

"Drowned." Jake's lips pressed together tightly. "Because she developed a taste for Oxygesic."

Kelly took a deep breath, trying to make sense of

Jake's words. Dan had deceived her by not telling her about his past. She'd become a convenient pawn in his investigation, just as she'd been a pawn in Brian's plan for moving up the corporate ladder.

Could it be? Her mind flashed on the old betrayal, Brian, and now, Dan.

She gripped the edge of the table, fighting the coffee clawing back up her throat.

Jake nodded as he pulled open the door to leave. "Just thought you should know."

GRAVEL CRUNCHED in Dan's driveway and he moved toward the door. Now what? Kelly pounded up the steps, moisture glistening in her eyes.

"I was going to pick you up—"

"How dare you." Deep pink splotches fired in her cheeks. "I trusted you. *Trusted you.* You lied to me from the moment I met you."

He reached for her, but she twisted away.

"Don't touch me."

Disbelief washed through him. "What are you talking about?"

"Jake came to see me." She pressed her lips into a thin line, her body trembling. "He told me the truth about your *corporate development.*"

His stomach pitched. So Jake had told her. Some friend. "Kelly, I—"

She held up a hand to silence him. "No more lies."

"What did he say?" Surprise and frustration rolled in his gut.

Kelly gestured wildly at the roofline of the house. "He told me you owe all this to your stock in Oxygesic." She leveled a fiery glare at him, her eyes full of hurt. "A drug you helped develop. You may as well have killed Diane yourself, isn't that right?"

The familiar pain tore at his heart. "I never meant to hurt anyone."

She laughed, a defeated, bitter burst of breath. "Well, you did." She bit down on her lip, obviously fighting to maintain control. "I believed you."

"Kelly." He reached for her again, but she pushed past him into the house. He spun around to follow her. "Do you have any idea of the hell I live with every day? Can you imagine how it feels to think I could be responsible for my own sister's death? For Rachel's death?"

"You deceived me," she interrupted.

Dan's frustration swelled to anger. "And what if I'd told you the truth? Would it have made a difference? Did you ever stop to think I might not have told you because my guilt is so thick I can barely breathe?"

He cupped her elbows in his hands, pulling her close. She didn't fight him, but squeezed her eyes shut. Silence stretched between them.

He refused to lose her. Not now. Not like this.

Her eyes flew open, anger flashing. "How do I know everything you've said to me isn't a lie?" She pulled free and grabbed his car keys from the hook next to the door. "I'm going to the meeting without you. Don't follow me."

"Kelly." He chased her to the steps, watching as she hurled the keys deep into the foliage.

She pivoted to face him. "I don't need you in my

life, and I don't need you to help me find out who killed Rachel." She swiped a hand beneath her damp eyes. "For all I know, you killed her. You and your Oxygesic."

Dan shook his head, frantically searching for a way to make her see the truth. To stop her. To convince her she was wrong. But she wasn't wrong. Oxygesic had killed Rachel—and Diane.

Kelly ran to her car then sped away from the house.

Dan snapped himself from his inner turmoil, racing back into his house for his spare keys. Panic teased at the edge of his consciousness.

Kelly might think she could go forward on her own, but she was on a collision course with the same fate that had met Rachel.

He had to stop her.

KELLY DROVE the three and a half hours toward the restaurant in silence. No radio. No music. No Dan. Just the sound of her mind berating her stupidity and naiveté.

She pulled the car into the Applebee's parking lot and glanced again at her handwritten note. Scott Jansen. Investigator for the state board of pharmacy. She checked her appearance in the visor mirror, took a deep breath and climbed from the car.

She hadn't come this far to walk away now. She was perfectly capable of getting to the bottom of Rachel's death without Dan's help. After all, he wasn't the only one with a guilty conscience to assuage.

She spotted a lone man in a far booth. He faced the door and nervously raked a hand through disheveled blond hair.

"Scott?"

He met her gaze, a forced smile straining his features. She pegged him as the type who looked a lot older than he was, probably the result of years spent frowning. "I was expecting Dan Steele."

"He couldn't make it." Kelly offered her hand. "Kelly Weir. I was a friend of Rachel's."

Jansen shook her hand, nodding toward the opposite side of the booth.

She sank onto the vinyl seat and took a deep breath. "I hope I didn't keep you waiting long."

"No problem." He stared at her for a long moment, measuring her with his dark gaze. Finally, he slid a thick folder across the table. "Thought this might help. Please don't tell anyone where you got it."

Kelly flipped open the cover, scrutinizing a printout of dates and items. "What am I looking at?"

"The C2 journal for Miller's Apothecary."

Kelly narrowed her eyes. "C2?"

"A class of narcotics. Includes Oxygesic." Jansen tapped the sheaf of paper. "Required documentation for C2s. This shows how many prescriptions the store filled and when. It matches their inventory as of our last inspection. No proof of any illegal activity."

She looked at him, confused. "So why are you giving this to me?"

"Gut feeling." He shrugged. "Years of experience." He took a sip of his soda.

Kelly suddenly realized her own mouth felt like the Sahara. She looked around, catching the eye of a middle-aged waitress.

"There's too much," Scott said flatly.

"Oxygesic?" She squinted at him and he nodded. "But what about Miller's proximity to the institute and the fact the other pharmacies near him don't carry the drug?"

"Mr. Steele said the same thing." Jansen frowned. "Who told you that?"

"Miller." Kelly's mind whirled. "I thought it was common knowledge."

"No." Jansen slowly shook his head. "Miller isn't the only pharmacy that carries Oxygesic. There are at least three others within a mile or two of his store. He's the only one who handles the institute's prescriptions. That's what doesn't make sense."

"He told me he was the only one, period." Kelly tensed.

The crease between Jansen's brows deepened. "He lied."

"But why?"

"So you wouldn't question his volume." He sat back against the bench seat. "It's way too high, but as long as he's got the records to match, there's not a whole lot we can do but wait and watch for him to slip up."

"Slip up?" Curiosity welled in Kelly's gut.

"If he's involved in selling the drug." Jansen lowered his voice. "Sooner or later someone will talk or the records won't match. He can't get away with it forever."

"What about the prescriptions?" Kelly flashed back to the young man paying cash—cash that had ended up in Miller's pocket. A second thought popped into her mind, this one of the good doctor. What if the two were partners? "How difficult is it to forge the prescriptions?"

Jansen nodded. "It's possible. But Miller's are all from the institute and legit."

The waitress slipped a glass of water in front of Kelly then took her order for a large mug of coffee. She and Scott sat in silence for a few moments.

"Sorry I'm late."

Kelly's heart slammed against her ribs when she heard Dan's voice.

He offered his hand to Scott. "Dan Steele. We spoke on the phone. I had some car trouble." He glared at Kelly then nodded at the seat next to her. "May I?"

She slid closer to the wall, wanting as much space as possible between her body and his. Her pulse pounded in her ears.

"What did I miss?" Dan asked.

Jansen filled Dan in on their conversation. Kelly watched as Dan scowled, steepling his fingers on the table as he listened.

"I don't understand why the authorities haven't stepped in," Dan said. "Have you reported this?"

"I tried," Jansen said. "State attorney's office told me I didn't have enough to go on. They said they'd notify the local sheriff's office there."

"Who also doesn't think there's enough to go on," Dan mumbled.

"So you've tried that route?" Jansen asked.

Dan nodded.

"Hopefully they're waiting and watching for Miller to make a mistake," Scott offered. He pushed the folder toward Kelly. "Keep that between us. I don't need to get fired over this." He threw a few dollars onto the table and stood to leave. "I need to get going."

"Thanks for meeting us." She patted the folder. "And for this. It's a big help."

"I never met Rachel," Scott said. "But if this guy killed her to save his hide, I'd like to see him fry."

HE POPPED the lock with ease and slipped into Kelly's house. This time he had come for the notes. It was time to stop the amateur sleuths in their tracks. No evidence. No problem.

He tossed a lamp for effect, smiling as the porcelain shattered.

He flipped open his pocketknife and gutted the sofa cushions one by one. Chunks of foam floated to the wood floor, but hid nothing.

The pale glow of a night-light shone at the end of the hall and he headed for the bedroom. If he knew little Miss Kelly Know-it-all, she'd have every bit of information she'd found filed, crossfiled and filed again.

He chuckled. It would be a cold day in hell before the northern babe pulled one over on him.

He was partway through the file search when he heard the wooden steps at the front of the house creak. He stepped behind the corner of the bedroom wall and waited. The noise sounded again.

"Kelly?" Helen Carroll's voice. "You home? You left the door wide-open." Footsteps. Coming down the hall. "Kelly?"

He raised the butt of his gun, waiting for her to clear the doorjamb.

Helen turned as she entered the bedroom, her eyes growing wide with fear and shock. "You," she mouthed.

He slammed the gun down on her skull. Her body sank to the floor, and he stared down at the lifeless heap. Most unfortunate.

He'd always liked the old lady, but she'd seen his face. What else could he do?

Chapter Twelve

Once Scott was gone, Kelly and Dan sat in silence.

His nearness was driving her insane, and she squirmed against the vinyl booth. "Why don't you move to the other side of the table?"

Dan leaned on one elbow, glaring at her. His eyebrows lifted. "I'm making you nervous?"

"Hardly." She sipped her coffee then took a long, deep breath. She pushed up from the table. "If you're not going to move, then get up so I can."

Dan stood, stepped around the table and slid into the opposite side of the booth, his features serious. "We're too close to solving this to be arguing now."

Kelly's stomach tightened. "Arguing? You're worried about arguing? You lied to me. Remember that part?"

His blue eyes pinned her then softened. He pushed the half-empty glass containing Scott's soda to the edge of the table. "I didn't think you'd help me if you knew the whole story. You're right."

He leaned forward, grabbing her hands before she could tug them free. His gaze bore into hers, challenging her. "But now, I care about you—and keeping you safe. I need you to believe me."

The heat of Kelly's anger and frustration flared in her cheeks. "I can't."

The feel of his warm, strong grip sent a shudder through her. She met his intent stare. Memories of Brian's deception swirled through her mind, battling with the contrast of Dan's intensity and nearness. Maybe the time had come to explain herself. After all, she finally understood Dan's true motivation.

She let out a quick breath and averted her gaze to their joined hands. "A year ago someone I thought I loved—someone I'd hoped to marry—betrayed me. Brian." Kelly lifted her gaze to Dan's. His deep blue eyes had softened. "My parents had died two years earlier and he'd comforted me. Loved me." A disbelieving laugh escaped from her lips. "I thought he'd loved me. We worked side by side at a large ad agency." She shook her head, still amazed at what had transpired. "He lifted my plans for several client campaigns."

She'd fought so hard to keep the memory shoved down that uttering the words squeezed at her chest. "He forwarded my work to competitors. Under my name. He made it look like I was selling company secrets."

Dan's gaze intensified. He tightened his grip on her hands. For a brief moment, Kelly realized she wanted him to never let go. Genuine concern flickered in the depths of his eyes, and she looked at the table once more, unwilling to process the emotion she'd seen.

"His *discovery* secured him one of the top slots at our agency. I'd been part of his master plan all along—right down to a phony engagement. I tried to fight him, but once your name's been smeared across the business section of the *Philadelphia Inquirer* it's difficult to convince people to listen to you."

"They went public with it?" Confusion tinged the deep timbre of Dan's voice.

Kelly steadied herself, then continued, "Rachel seized the opportunity to do a piece for the paper." Kelly's focus found Dan's kind gaze once more and locked there. Traitorous heat blossomed in her chest. "She knew I'd been set up, but she said the story was too good to pass up. She thought I'd forgive her."

"But you didn't."

Kelly blinked back the moisture welling in her eyes as she looked at Dan. "I'm not very good at the whole forgiveness thing. My parents were big believers in the art of grudge-holding." She tipped up her chin, hoping she could fight back her tears before they spilled over her lashes. "Hey, it got her national recognition. At my expense."

Dan opened his mouth to speak, but Kelly shook her head. He pressed his lips closed and remained silent.

Kelly drew in a slow, steadying breath. "Rachel tried to apologize, but I never returned a single call or letter. Years of friendship, down the drain. Maybe I was too quick to throw it all away, but it hurt. It still hurts."

"Why did you come here to pack up her things?" Dan asked.

Kelly shrugged. "It seemed like the right thing to do. Packing up her life represented closure to me." Her voice dropped low. "And now solving the mystery of her death is something I need to do. I ignored her for a year and lost her. I won't ignore her now."

"I'm sorry." Dan's voice quavered, as if the carefully guarded emotion he kept bottled inside threatened to overflow.

For a brief moment Kelly wanted to lose herself—in the comforting tone of his voice and in the strong touch of his fingers clasped around hers. But she couldn't. Not this time.

She jerked her hands free just as his cell phone rang.

"Damn." He pulled the phone from his pocket. "Steele."

His eyes grew wide, the color draining from his cheeks as he listened.

"Is she all right? When did it start?" He stood, pulling his wallet from his pocket and tossing a ten-dollar bill onto the table. "I'm on my way."

Kelly straightened, her heart in her throat. "What's happened?"

"It's my mother." His vivid gaze had dimmed, shadowed by panic. "She's having a psychotic episode. I need to go."

"I'm sorry." As upset with him as she'd been, her heart twisted at the worry etched across Dan's face.

He pointed at her as he stepped away from the table. "Don't think this conversation is finished."

Kelly watched as he raced out of the restaurant back toward Summer Shores. Her heart sank, acid rising in her throat.

She knew the conversation was far from over, but she wasn't sure she had the strength for round two.

MADDIE LAY in her bed, her skin tissue-paper thin and pale. Her lips moved, but the words she uttered were barely audible. "Candy Man. Stop him. Killing her. Candy Man."

"Momma." Moisture blurred Dan's vision as he pulled up a chair and stroked his mother's forehead. She didn't deserve this thing called Alzheimer's. No one did. "I'm here, Momma. You're okay. I won't let anyone hurt you."

"Candy Man."

"She's sedated now." The supervisor spoke softly over Dan's shoulder. "I think she'll sleep through the night."

"I'm glad you called me." Dan stood to face the nurse. "What set her off? Do you know?"

"She was staring out the window in the activity room." The woman rubbed her hand across tired-looking eyes. "Like she always does. She just stares at the sound."

"I know." Dan turned back toward his mother's still figure. "She always talks about this Candy Man. Does it make any sense to you?"

The woman shook her head and smiled. "I'm sorry to say most of what these folks say doesn't make any sense." She patted Dan's shoulder. "It's the nature of the disease."

DAN'S WORDS rattled through Kelly's mind during the entire drive home. Could she forgive him? After all, his intentions had been far more pure than Brian's or Rachel's.

She had promised herself she'd never fall into the trap of truly caring for someone again, but she had. For Dan. As hurt as she'd been, she still cared far more than she wanted to admit.

What if he was telling the truth about how he felt? Her insides caught at the thought. What if he was the man who could complete her, make her whole? If she walked away from him now, she'd never know.

Kelly squinted, refocusing on the road as she neared her street. She turned, easing the car onto the narrow lane then into her driveway, nearly running over Edgar.

She swerved onto the lawn and slammed the car into Park, scrambling out of her seat. "Edgar. I could have killed you."

The cat paced and circled in the center of the drive, yowling frantically.

The small hairs at the back of Kelly's neck pricked to attention. She glanced at Helen's house. The front door sat wide-open.

"Helen," she whispered. She raced across the street, fear coursing through her, snapping her senses to life.

She burst through the door and ran from room to room. Helen was nowhere to be found. The television set played to an empty living room. Where could the woman be? Kelly glanced around, expecting Edgar to be behind her, but he hadn't followed. She dashed back into the street. The tomcat continued to circle and yowl in Kelly's driveway.

"What the—" The sight of her own front door sitting open turned her veins to ice. What if Miller had come calling and Helen had walked in on him?

Kelly took the steps two at a time and tore into the house. The living room lamp lay shattered on the floor, shards of porcelain spread wide. The sofa cushions had been slashed and gutted, foam pieces scattered over every inch of the hardwood floor.

"Helen." Panic seized her now, but she rushed forward toward the bedroom, pulling her cell phone from her pocket.

Rachel's file cabinet lay tipped on its side, her papers strewn across the room. The French doors were ajar. Kelly choked back tears, her fear for Helen overwhelming her senses.

She dialed 911 and waited. As she did, her gaze fell to a dark stain on the rug just inside the door. Her heart lurched. *Helen.*

"State your emergency," the dispatcher answered.

"My home has been ransacked and my neighbor may be injured. I can't find her. I think someone's attacked her. Abducted her. I don't know." Her voice had grown monotone and robotic. In a daze, she walked slowly down the hall, listening for the dispatcher's response.

"I need you to give me the address and stay on the line," the dispatcher stated calmly. "Do not go in the house."

"I'm in the house," Kelly mumbled. A lone tear tumbled down her cheek, and she swiped it away. My God. Who had done this? Miller? The fine hairs along the back of her neck lifted, icy cold fear whispering through her veins. Was he outside some-where? Watching? Had he killed Helen as he'd killed Rachel?

Kelly choked, a sharp sob racking her body.

"I need you to go outside and wait by the curb."

"But my neighbor…" Kelly's gaze fell on the spiral staircase. Could Helen be there? Could Miller be there? Waiting for her? Lurking in the darkness?

Her knees wobbled and she clutched at the railing to steady herself.

"A unit is on its way. Please do as I ask."

Kelly numbly walked to the porch and down to the drive. Edgar wound his way between her calves. She scooped him into the curve of her arm. "It's okay, sweetie," she cooed. "She's got to be okay."

Dread puddled deep inside her. If Helen were anywhere nearby, Edgar would be at her side. So where was she? And what had happened?

"Are you still there, Miss?" the dispatcher asked.

"I'm here. I'm outside."

What had she done? Had her investigation brought harm to Helen? She'd never be able to forgive herself. A siren wailed in the distance, growing closer with each passing second. Kelly leaned against her car, waiting and praying her friend would be all right.

SIRENS FIRED in the distance, growing louder as Dan talked to the nursing supervisor. For a fleeting moment he wondered what had happened, but turned again to his mother, retaking his seat.

A second nurse appeared in the doorway, tapping

lightly on the jamb. "Madge. Something's going on in the marsh."

"What do you mean?" the supervisor asked.

"Cops are everywhere. Two kids found someone half-dead in the bushes."

The supervisor clasped a hand over her mouth. Dan's heart caught, and unease tightened his insides. Had Kelly gotten home safely? It couldn't be her, could it? He should have never left her at the restaurant alone. What if she'd been followed?

"The detective's in the activities room. He wanted to speak with the person in charge. He needs to question anyone that might have seen something."

Dan looked at his mother's lips, still uttering the words "Candy Man" over and over. "You don't think?"

The supervisor shook her head. "No. It's a coincidence. She's been saying that for weeks." She stepped to where the second nurse waited. "If you'll excuse me."

Dan's mother had fallen silent. A sense of urgency welled inside him. He had to speak to the detective in charge—had to find out who'd been attacked.

He pressed his lips against Maddie's cool forehead. "I love you, Momma," he whispered against her smooth skin.

Once out in the hall he glanced toward the activities room. Aides and nurses flitted in and out. The hall buzzed with conversations about the discovery made just steps outside their windows. Dan's gut clenched when Jake stepped out of the activities room and into the hall.

"Danny," he called out. "What brings you here?"

Dan jerked his thumb toward his mother's room as he strode toward his friend. "Mom had a rough day. What's going on?"

"Someone attacked Helen Carroll, that's what."

Dan leaned against the wall for support. "Helen? How? When?"

Jake shook his head. "We don't know. I can't imagine who would want to hurt her and dump her here."

"How is she?"

"Alive. Barely. They took her to Memorial."

"Why here?"

Jake grasped Dan's shoulder. "We think someone took her from Kelly's house."

Fear gripped Dan's insides and twisted. Hard. He scrutinized Jake's features. "Kelly?"

"She's okay. There's a unit there now and the crime-scene guys are on their way."

"What happened?"

"She found the place ransacked. Called it in. Said she couldn't find Helen, and the cat was going nuts." He gestured toward the activities room's bank of windows. "Couple of teens stumbled across Helen's body. Nick of time, too. Any longer and she wouldn't have had a chance."

"Was this meant for Kelly?" Even as he spoke the words, Dan silently urged Jake to say no. *Not Kelly.*

Jake nodded. "It's too soon to know for sure. But my gut says yes. It's time to go after Miller."

Dan's fear morphed into anger. "What took you so long, Jake? Did you have to wait for someone to be seriously hurt?"

Jake arched one brow, a guilty expression settling across his stern features. "I'll make it right." He pushed against Dan's shoulder. "Get going. Kelly's probably scared to death."

Panic rose in Dan's throat as he ran for the exit, headed toward Kelly's house.

I'll make it right. Jake's words echoed in Dan's mind. Miller's violence had escalated. It was too late to make things right. All Dan could do now was pray they'd be able to make him stop before he struck again.

Chapter Thirteen

Flashing lights slashed through the pines as Dan turned onto Fourth Avenue. His heart twisted at the sight of the police cruiser in Kelly's drive. *Kelly.*

Had Miller intended to silence Kelly, but beaten poor Helen instead?

He pulled the car onto the lawn across the street and ran toward the house. Kelly sat on the bottom step, Edgar wrapped in her arms.

"Are you all right?" Fear churned through him. What if she hadn't gone to meet Jansen? Would she be the one in a hospital bed fighting for her life? Or worse?

She stood, the lights from the police cruiser catching the sheen of tears on her cheeks. Dan stopped short in front of her as a sob racked her shoulders. His relief and fear battled, welling in his throat until he choked on the depth of the emotions.

Pulling Kelly into his arms, he stroked her hair, relishing the feel of her body safe within his embrace. Edgar let out a meow, but settled quietly between them.

After a few moments, Dan held Kelly at arm's length, taking in the sight of her. "Are you hurt at all?"

She shook her head, biting back another sob. "Did he kill her? There was blood."

"She's at the hospital," Dan said softly. "Some kids found her in the marsh. She's hurt pretty badly."

Kelly's eyes grew wide. Her lips parted then closed again, as if words defied her.

"Let me find the officer in charge." Dan glanced toward the house. "I'll take you to her so you can be there when she wakes up."

Kelly nodded, her eyes dazed, her throat working. He ran his thumb across her cheek to swipe away the moisture, overwhelmed again by his need to protect her. "Whoever did this tonight will never lay a hand on you. You hear me?"

She nodded.

"I'll be right back." He headed up the steps, hoping Kelly hadn't heard the desperation in his voice.

HOURS LATER, Kelly sat at Helen's bedside, cradling the woman's frail hand in her own. Wires ran from Helen's chest to monster machines on either side of the bed. The ventilator tube whooshed life into her tiny body.

Exhaustion seeped through Kelly, but she fought sleep, wanting to be awake when Helen came to. *If* she came to. *No.* She caught herself, rewording the thought. *When* she came to.

Helen's face swam beyond the tears filling Kelly's eyes. How could she have any tears left? She rarely cried, but hadn't been able to stop since last night. Not since she'd seen Dan across the driveway. The enormity of her feelings for him had shaken her to her core. And the tears had started.

She needed him—with every fiber of her being. The thought scared her to death. Kelly had been shocked by his link to Oxygesic, but the revelation explained the primal intensity always simmering just below the surface of his control. She needed to proceed carefully, but for now, she'd work alongside him. She felt safer there than anywhere else.

She refocused on Helen, grimacing at the sight of her pale face. If anyone could recover from such a brutal attack, she could. After all, she was one tough old bird—in her own words. Kelly had grown to love the outspoken sweetheart as if she were her own grandmother.

Miller. Kelly shook her head, rubbing a hand across her tired eyes. No matter what he had done in the past, she couldn't believe him capable of violence against someone so frail. Helen was no threat to him. Why would he go after her? Simply because she'd seen his face?

Kelly stroked Helen's cheek, hoping the poor thing could sense her healing prayers.

The morning sun blinked through the blinds, and Kelly glanced at her watch. A little before seven.

"Hey." Dan's voice sounded softly next to her shoulder. The aroma of fresh coffee tickled her nose. "Brought you something."

Kelly stood to stretch her legs, taking the offered cup. "Thanks."

"How you holding up?"

"No complaints." She gave a weak smile. "How will she ever recover from this?" Tears threatened again, but she blinked them back.

He cupped her chin, brushing his thumb lightly across her cheek. The now familiar gesture warmed her, soothing her wounded spirit. "She will. Trust me. I've known Helen for a long time."

Kelly leaned into his touch, wanting nothing more than to curl up in his arms. "This is my fault." Regret settled heavily in her stomach.

Dan shook his head, shushing her. "It's Miller's fault. No one else's."

Dan's expression shifted, growing intent. "Jake needs to speak with us. Are you up to going to his office?"

Kelly nodded wearily, casting a nervous glance toward Helen. "I don't want to leave her alone, though."

"Marge Healey's outside. She'll sit with her until we get back."

"Where's Edgar?"

"At my house, probably trashing the place as we speak. He wasn't too happy about being shut inside." He patted her shoulder. "Come on. The sooner we go, the sooner we'll get you back."

Kelly stepped to the bed, kissed her fingertips then pressed them to Helen's forehead. She turned back to Dan, holding her chin high. "Let's go."

"I'M NOT GOING to lie to you." Jake ran a hand over the stubble of his beard. "I didn't think the guy would escalate like this. I knew he was a concern, but this?" He hung his head, rearranging a pile of papers on his desk.

Kelly and Dan sat facing him, impatience growing in Kelly's gut as she glanced from Dan's stern expression back to Jake. "Have you arrested him yet?"

Jake met her gaze. Dark circles smudged the flesh beneath his eyes. "Not yet. I don't want to rush. No mistakes."

"What can we do to help?" Dan straightened, his voice strong and determined.

Jake pushed back from his chair and sat on the corner of the desk. "I need your notes. Whatever you've found." He rubbed his neck then stretched his back. "Unless that's what Miller got last night."

Kelly snapped to attention, her pulse quickening. "Is that why he trashed my house?"

"Probably." Jake scowled.

"They were with me." She shook her head. "Everything's in my car."

"We went to meet someone from the state pharmacy board," Dan explained.

Jake shook his head, obviously not pleased they'd gone against his request. His jaw tightened then released. "Regardless, I'll need everything you have."

"I can be back in a half hour." Kelly scraped back her chair.

Dan stood, interrupting her before she could stand. "No, I'll take you back to Helen. I'll go get the notes and run them back. You should be with Helen when she wakes up."

Jake brightened. "So they think she'll regain consciousness soon?"

Kelly lowered her face into her hands, blowing out an exhausted sigh. "We just don't know."

Dan shot a glance at Kelly. Her elbows sat braced on her knees, her face buried in her palms. He looked at Jake, giving a quick shake of his head. "It's too soon to tell."

Jake nodded his understanding and shook Dan's hand. "Any help you can give us would be appreciated."

"I'm on it." Dan reached for Kelly's hand, bracing one arm around her waist as he walked her out into the hall. His concern about her physical state deepened. If anything happened now, she'd be too tired to think straight. "You've got to sleep."

"Can't." Her voice shook with determination. "I won't sleep until Miller's locked up and they tell us Helen's out of the woods."

SEVERAL HOURS later, Dan stood in the cool autumn sunshine, watching as a pair of uniformed officers brought Miller out of his store in cuffs. The slime hung his head. Anger boiled deep in Dan's chest.

The coward couldn't meet the accusing stares of gathered onlookers, but he could assault a frail, elderly woman until the only things keeping her alive were machines.

"It's over." Jake walked to his side.

"Good evidence?" Hope simmered in Dan's belly.

"This is between me and you." Jake glanced around quickly, making sure they were out of earshot from any bystanders. "How does a ledgerful of illegal drug profits and photos matching those found in Kelly's house sound?"

Dan's smile spread wide. "Sounds like a slam-dunk conviction by a jury of his peers."

"How about a duffel bag of cash?" Jake added, one blond brow lifting. "Or a rifle, well hidden, but probably used to take a shot at the cemetery."

Dan narrowed his eyes. "Why so careless? How did he get away with this so long if he was that stupid?"

"Maybe he was planning on leaving town in a hurry." Jake shook his head. "We must have made our move just in time."

"What about Rachel's death?"

"Don't worry. If Miller did it, we'll get it out of him." Jake slapped a hand on Dan's shoulder. "Go tell Kelly she's safe."

"I will." Dan's voice dropped to a mutter. "Too bad I can't say the same to Helen."

DAN STOOD in the doorway, watching quietly. Kelly had pulled her chair tight to Helen's bed. Apparently their elderly friend's condition hadn't changed, but Kelly had fallen asleep, bent at the waist, forehead resting on Helen's bed.

His stomach caught and twisted at the sight of her, the full force of his feelings for her slamming him like a sucker punch. They hadn't revisited yesterday's argument. Though now was hardly the time.

He kneeled next to her, whispering as he brushed a long, auburn curl from her face, "I'm taking you home."

Her swollen eyes blinked open and she smiled. "Is she awake?" She pulled herself upright, gazing eagerly at Helen. Her features fell slack at the sight of the unchanged position and the whoosh of the ventilator.

"Sorry." Dan put his hands on her shoulders and squeezed, consumed by the desire to keep her safe, to shelter her from Miller. She needed to regain her strength if he was going to do either. "You've got to get some sleep. Let's go."

"What if she wakes up?"

"They'll call us." He held out his hand. "Come on."

Kelly stood on wobbly legs. Dan wrapped an arm around her waist, pulling her close, breathing deep her fresh scent.

"What happened to Vince?" Her eyes brightened.

"He's in custody. They found plenty of evidence." Dan kissed her hair, letting his lips linger for a moment against the silky strands. "We got him."

Her weight shifted, and he grew suddenly aware of her soft curves pressed to his chest.

"Thank God," she whispered, looking up, her deep brown gaze searching his face.

Dan angled his mouth over hers, drinking in the warmth of her lips. She wound her arms around his neck, twisting her fingers into his hair.

"I'm sorry I dragged you into all of this." He spoke the words slowly, whispering them against her mouth.

Kelly pulled back. Dan read forgiveness and what he hoped was desire, deep in her eyes, as they locked with his.

"It's over now." Her tone rang heavy with fatigue and relief. "Let's go home."

EDGAR'S YOWLING had ceased from outside the bedroom door. Kelly had given him an entire can of tuna, proving that anyone's silence could be bought.

Dan sat back against the pillows, watching as she peeled her sweater over her head. Her hair tumbled about her shoulders and the glow of twilight through the shutters illuminated her pale skin.

The juxtaposition of Helen's attack and Miller's arrest had filled him with a desire to lose himself with Kelly. He needed to hold her, to escape from the reality of all that had happened, if only for a little while.

He pulled her onto his lap, comforted by her fluid movements as she wrapped her legs around his waist. Desire flooded his body, gathering in a pool of heat where her jeans pressed against his.

He traced his lips across the soft flesh at the base of her neck then down to the warm cleavage between her breasts. A moan escaped her lips and he smiled against her skin. He tugged the soft fabric of her bra into his mouth, flicking his tongue across one pert nipple.

He took his time. Kissing. Caressing. Teasing.

Kelly reached behind her back, unfastening her bra and dropping it to the floor. Even in the semidark room, the beauty of her curves, the flush of her skin and the warmth of her body overwhelmed him.

Dan rolled her onto her back, drawing the sides of his fingers across each breast, cupping one and then the other. "So beautiful." And she was. More beautiful than anyone or anything he'd ever seen.

Kelly arched her back, pressing her body into his touch. He trailed his fingers to the waist of her jeans, freeing the button that held them closed. He pulled down the zipper to slip his fingers between the denim and the soft, moist satin of her panties.

She murmured his name, rocking her body against his caress.

Dan shifted, lowering Kelly gently to the bed, pulling her jeans and panties down the length of her legs and over her feet. He pressed a kiss to her ankle, then teased and suckled slowly up her creamy calf, to the curve of her knee, then inside her thigh. Her fingers wound into his hair, her body straining to meet his approaching lips.

He touched his tongue lightly to her swollen heat. She trembled beneath him as he tasted and explored. He wanted to sample every inch of her body, every corner of her soul, focused solely on loving her now that she was safe.

Kelly shuddered and moaned, her body twisting with pleasure. Dan slipped two fingers into her warmth, never stopping the slow, soft movements of his tongue. The contractions of her release were immediate.

Dan smiled against her silken skin as he pressed his lips to her belly. It delighted him that he could give her such pleasure…and that she was his.

The explosion of her orgasm was like nothing Kelly had ever known. The room spun as she tried to raise her head from the pillow to look at Dan. Splinters of light flashed in the periphery of her vision and she trembled uncontrollably. She reached for Dan's shoulders, pulling at him.

She wanted him inside her, needed the reassuring joining of their bodies. Helen's attack had left Kelly devastated and afraid, but Dan's strength and caresses had infused her with a calm assurance they'd be all right. Finally.

His weight shifted away from her and the nightstand drawer slid open. She heard the rip of foil as Dan took her hand. "Help me."

She pushed herself onto one elbow, taking the condom from him. She paused to run her palm down the length of his erect shaft. She wrapped her fingers around him and lovingly stroked.

Dan's eyes closed, his head tipping backward. She gently reversed the direction of her touch, caressing her way up his rock-hard length.

He caught her hand in his, his eyes flashing open to meet her gaze. The intensity of his stare sent excitement surging through her. Desire arced between them, fed by a mutual need like nothing she'd ever experienced before.

Kelly rolled the condom down the length of his erection then lay down on top of him, lightly trailing the tips of her fingernails down his muscled chest, grinning with pleasure as he groaned.

She pressed her lips to his flesh, flicking her tongue across one flat nipple. His breath caught and she grinned again, intent on giving him as much pleasure as he had given her.

She ran her tongue slowly down the middle of his stomach and stopped mere inches from where he throbbed, waiting for release. She lifted herself above him and guided him gently between her legs.

She held her breath as he filled her. Dan's head pressed back against the pillow, his eyes closed.

"Kelly," he murmured.

The sound of her name on his lips pushed her desire to the edge.

He cupped the cheeks of her buttocks, rocking her slowly at first, then with increasing urgency. He buried his face in her breasts, taking one nipple and the surrounding soft flesh into his mouth, pulling and caressing.

Kelly cried out as a second wave of release tore through her.

Dan swiftly rolled her beneath him, his hands indenting the soft covers on either side of her. She closed her eyes, savoring the feel of their bodies moving as one.

"Look at me," he whispered. "I want to see your eyes."

She snapped open her eyes, thrilling to the depth of longing shining in his gaze. Her focus never left his as he shuddered and groaned, his chin dropping to his chest.

In that one vulnerable moment, she forgave him for lying about his past, wanting only to lose herself in the vitality he'd sparked to life deep within her.

The waves of his release pulsed through her before his body relaxed, his cheek pressing momentarily to her own. Every ounce of tension fled her exhausted body as he feathered kisses along her neck and across her shoulder.

"I love you, Dan." Fatigue overtook her as she thought the words, wondering for a fleeting moment if she'd murmured them out loud as she slipped into a long, deep sleep.

HE CRUSHED the tablet between two spoons, letting the powder fall onto the gravy of the meatball sandwich. The flakes vanished, dissolving into the steaming tomato sauce.

He rewrapped the foil, gripping the sandwich in his fist. One more piece. Miller was just one more piece of the puzzle to be taken care of.

The pharmacist's eyes grew wide as he entered the cell.

"Dinner."

Miller took the offered package and sat back on the cot. He unwrapped the foil then looked up. "I didn't know you cared."

"I don't."

"You need to make these charges go away."

He shrugged. Like he'd ever let Miller tell him what to do. "Natives aren't too crazy about you assaulting Helen Carroll."

Miller snorted with a grin, his blue eyes icier than normal. "You know I had nothing to do with that. I'm not the violent one in this arrangement."

He narrowed his eyes and spoke slowly, evenly. "Evidence says you did. Seems to me, I'm in complete control of your future. Maybe you've had a free ride for too long."

"Free ride?" Miller climbed to his feet, his cool demeanor vanishing. "You call this a free ride?"

"If you're so unhappy with the way things are, you could be replaced."

"What is that? A threat?"

A long silence beat between them.

"If I go down, I'm taking you with me," Miller added.

"I wouldn't be too sure about that." He shoved Miller back onto the cot and turned to leave the cell. "Enjoy your sandwich."

Chapter Fourteen

Kelly rolled out of bed as the dawn's light filtered through the window. She gathered her clothes, strewn across the floor, and slipped out into the hall to the bathroom. Her familiar inner turmoil had returned, magnified by how intimate her lovemaking with Dan had been.

She'd been devastated by the attack on Helen, and had sought solace in his arms. He'd done the same, but the reality was that with every intimate step they took, he sank deeper and deeper beneath her skin. She'd allowed herself to become vulnerable, heart and soul. The realization frightened her.

After she'd freshened and dressed, she padded barefoot to the kitchen where Edgar circled his empty food bowl. "You've got a one-track mind." She scooped the feline into her arms to plant a kiss on the top of his head and give him a squeeze. He purred like a small engine, rubbing his chin against hers.

"Okay, Your Highness." Kelly set him down on his paws. "More tuna, coming right up."

Once Edgar had settled happily with his full bowl and Kelly had wrapped her fingers around a steaming mug of coffee, she pulled open the sliding door and stepped into the damp, cool morning. A heavy sea breeze had coated the windows and deck furniture with a patina of moisture. Kelly wiped the seat of a chair with her sleeve and sat.

The ocean was calm, giving no indication of the fury the town had experienced. She took a long sip, grimacing as the hot beverage slid down her throat.

Her thoughts slipped back to Dan. What had she done? She'd fallen for a man she barely knew, in a town in which she had no intention of staying. Regret settled heavily in her bones. She needed to go home.

Her heart twisted in protest.

Dan brought sensations and emotions out in her that she had never felt before, even though she hadn't intended to feel anything—for anyone—ever again.

Yet he'd lied about his previous relationship with Rachel and about his role in Oxygesic. Kelly tapped her foot on the deck—the deck purchased with stock profits from the company responsible for the drug.

What else had he lied about? She'd be a fool to stay.

She got up to leave but stopped short when she turned for the door. Dan stood, one arm propped against the slider, watching her. His features were grim, as if he sensed her decision. Her stomach tilted on its side.

"Where are you off to in such a hurry?" He closed the space between them, tucking a strand of hair behind her ear then cupping her chin.

"I'm leaving." Kelly took a step backward.

"To go back to the hospital?"

She shook her head, struggling one last time with the choice she was about to make—the choice she had to make. "I'm going home to Philadelphia."

Dan's eyes grew wide, his features hardening. "You told me you loved me."

Her breath caught. So she *had* spoken the words out loud. *Fool.* "I'm sorry."

Kelly moved to step past him, but he grabbed her arm. "I made a mistake. Why won't you look past that?"

"I can't." She shook her head, stepping quickly into the living room.

Dan's footsteps fell close on her heels.

She hurried toward the kitchen, something breaking deep inside her.

He grabbed her by the shoulders, turning her to face him. "I'd like to get my hands around the throat of the man who did this to you."

His features twisted in anger, and Kelly's heart hammered in her chest. "You're scaring me."

He released his grip, fury gleaming in his eyes. "I never wanted to need anyone, Kelly, but I need you."

She rinsed out her mug and squared her shoulders, knowing how much it had taken for him to admit his feelings. "I'm leaving as soon as Helen is out of the woods."

"That's not acceptable to me." Anger tinged his words.

Kelly stared at him, dazed by what he'd said. She steadied her breathing and chose her own words carefully. "This isn't about what's acceptable to you."

His shoulders dropped. The familiar shadow crossed his face, tucking away the emotion that had momentarily escaped. "I'll drive you to the hospital."

"I'll walk. I want to pick up my car." She nodded toward Edgar, who sat quizzically observing their exchange. "Can he stay here until I get the house cleaned up?"

"No problem." Dan's features softened. "You can stay, too, if you'd like."

She met his gaze head-on. "I don't belong here."

KELLY SAT in the middle of Rachel's living room. Boxes lay scattered across the floor, a roll of bubble wrap by her side. She had put this task off long enough. After all, this was the reason she'd come to Summer Shores in the first place, wasn't it? She'd come to pack up Rachel's life. Nothing more. One last attempt to reconcile with the friend she'd shut out at the end of her life.

Kelly sighed. She was glad Miller was in jail, glad Helen would recover, but devastated Rachel was gone. It had taken days to hit her, but now it had. Hard.

She'd called the hospital when she'd gotten home from Dan's. The floor nurse had explained Helen was breathing on her own but still unconscious. Kelly had decided to spend some time packing, hoping a little physical work would ease her frustration and heartache over Dan.

She'd told the nurse she'd be in a bit later, after

stopping off to thank Jake Arnold for apprehending Miller.

Closing her eyes, Kelly imagined Dan's arms around her, holding her close after they had made love. Her curves had fit the smooth planes of his body as though they were made for each other. Skin to skin. Heart to heart. Brushing a tear from her cheek, she decided it was better to focus on her work than on something she could never have.

She grabbed the roll of packing tape and struggled to pull it tight across the flaps of a box. She hated this stuff. Always had. The tape twisted, sticking to itself, and she tugged hard against the cutting edge.

The roll flew out of her hand, landing against the wall. Kelly crawled to retrieve it, stretching flat on her belly to avoid climbing around the piles she'd made. Her fingers snagged the edge of the roll.

"Got you, you little—"

Her gaze flickered to the space behind the bookcase and the edge of something deep in the shadows.

She pulled herself to her knees to scramble closer. Her arm barely fit into the tight space but she was able to touch the object. The spine of a book. *Odd.* Most of Rachel's books had been kept near her desk in the bedroom.

She stood, struggling to wiggle the mammoth bookcase a few inches from the wall. She dropped to her knees and pulled the book free. It wasn't dusty, so it couldn't have been back there terribly long. Kelly turned it in her hands to examine the cover. Blank. The dust jacket missing.

She glanced at the spine. *The Complete Works of William Shakespeare.*

Her breath caught, and she dropped onto her heels. Shakespeare. The mysterious single word in Rachel's notebook.

Kelly pulled open the front cover only to find the insides hollowed out. The book was a fake designed to hide secrets—or papers in this case.

Slipping her fingers beneath the sheets of paper, she pulled them free. Journal pages listed a dizzying log of dates, names and dollar amounts. Could this be part of Miller's journal, the one Jake had found in the pharmacy?

A small sheet of notebook paper sat shoved in the middle of the pages. On it, someone had scribbled a single word. *Arnold.* The handwriting looked like Rachel's, but the letters had been made in a frenzied scrawl.

Kelly climbed to her feet, carrying the papers to the sofa. She sank onto the cushion and pushed her hair out of her face.

Arnold? What did Jake have to do with any of this? Maybe he had been Rachel's next step? Maybe she had been ready to go to him with her notes when she'd been killed?

Kelly looked up at the bookcase. Rachel must have hidden the notes here before she mailed Kelly the key to the post-office box. She returned the notes to their hollow in the book and closed the cover. Smart. Rachel had always been smart.

Kelly slipped the book and its contents into her backpack. She'd drop off them off at Jake's office on her way to the hospital. Maybe then he'd be able to ensure Miller never hurt anyone again.

"HE'S DEAD," Jake said.

"Dead? Miller?" Dan pulled his car to the side of the road to concentrate on Jake's call, disbelief surging through him. "How? When?"

"Killed himself in his cell. Figures he'd take the easy way out."

Dan rubbed a hand across his face. "What's easy about killing yourself?"

"Looked like a baby sleeping. Took something. Typical." Dan could hear Jake's snarl through the phone. "Too weak to face the music. Denied it right up until the end. Never did like the guy."

"Preaching to the choir." Dan blinked, unable to fully wrap his brain around this latest turn of events. "I'll tell Kelly."

He disconnected then punched in Kelly's number. The phone rang and rang. No answer. She must not have turned the machine back on after Miller's threatening messages. He tried her cell, but still got no answer. He frowned. She couldn't have left town, could she? His stomach caught. No. She'd never leave before Helen was well.

He needed to apologize for his behavior this morning. He couldn't blame her for her doubts. Hell, he had doubts of his own. After she'd left, he'd had time to think about everything that had transpired between them.

They'd been swept up in their investigation, connecting on emotional and physical levels. He couldn't help but question how long a connection like that would last in the real word. Maybe it was better if she left now, before everyday life pulled them apart.

He tensed, knowing his heart didn't believe a word he'd thought. Regardless, he had to find her to tell her about Miller.

Dead. As much as he despised Miller, Dan could hardly believe it. Something didn't add up.

Why would someone professing his innocence kill himself?

Dan pulled the car back onto the road, pressing the accelerator flat to the floor. He'd leave that question to the pros. All he wanted to do now was find Kelly to tell her Miller would never intimidate or harm anyone again.

"SORRY TO KEEP you waiting." Jake confidently strode into his office, owning the space, his expression sharp.

Kelly reached to shake his hand.

"Bit of excitement today in the holding area," he continued. "Miller."

"What about him?"

Jake sank into his chair. "I'm guessing he took something. We won't know until the autopsy comes back."

Kelly gripped the arms of her chair, her stomach rolling. "He's dead?"

"As a doornail."

Her heart hammered against her ribs. Could it be over, just like that? "How?"

"We never thought he was a suicide risk." Jake shook his head. "We didn't search him closely enough."

"Suicide?" Kelly's pulse pounded in her temples. Between Jake's nonchalance and the news of Miller's death, her senses were on overload. "Miller seemed too arrogant for suicide."

Jake shrugged. "I guess getting caught erased some of his bravado."

Kelly's mind raced. Would Miller kill himself rather than try to prove his innocence? Was the evidence that compelling? If anything, Kelly would have thought he'd secretly savor the notoriety.

"Kelly?"

Jake's voice jarred her from her jumbled thoughts. "Pardon?"

He held a hard candy in an outstretched hand. "I asked if you wanted a candy?"

Kelly reached for the morsel. "Sure. Thanks." She unwrapped the cellophane and popped the candy into her mouth.

"Root beer." Jake winked. "My favorite."

"Thanks," she said distractedly. "I came to thank you for going after Miller. For getting him off of the street."

Jake laughed. Kelly shivered, a chill permeating her bones. For some reason, Jake's reactions seemed off today.

"Now that he's dead, your worries are over." Jake stood, fists on hips. "I guess you'll be going home."

"Guess so." Kelly took a deep breath, preparing to ask the question she desperately needed answered, for her own peace of mind. "Do you think he killed Rachel?"

Jake nodded. "You should have seen how much money he was making. Her story was a threat to him. He'd have lost everything."

"And now he's dead." Kelly frowned, trying to make sense of all that had happened in the past few days. "What about the opiate in Rachel's system? How would he do that?"

A blond brow arched. "Forced it down her throat at gunpoint? Might work."

The quickness of his answer surprised her, but, after all, he was the cop. "What about Diane?"

"We'll never know. It may have been Miller, or it may have been an accident." Jake lifted a framed photo from the credenza behind his desk.

Diane. Kelly recognized her from Dan's photo. "She was beautiful." Her heart ached for Jake and for Dan, both having lost someone they loved.

"Very special." Jake's voice had gone soft. He set the frame on his desk, tracing a finger across the captured image. "This was one of the last photos I took of her."

His words piqued Kelly's interest, her pulse quickening. "You're a photographer?"

"Very amateur." He met her gaze. "Haven't shot a thing in so long, I doubt I'd remember how." A melancholy laugh slipped from his lips. "Hell, back in the day I developed my own shots."

"Like Miller," Kelly whispered.

Jake's features fell slack, his cold gaze piercing through her. Fear simmered in her gut, and she fingered the zipper of her backpack, thinking of the book and notes inside.

Arnold.

Maybe Rachel hadn't planned to tell Arnold. Maybe she'd discovered Jake Arnold had been the one with everything to lose, not Vince Miller.

"I'm nothing like Miller," Jake snarled. "I can assure you I'm much smarter than he ever was."

Kelly shook off the shudder his words caused, standing to leave. "I'm sure you've got a lot of paperwork to get through. I won't take up any more of your time."

She walked to the end of the hall then stopped, waiting just around the corner. As she had hoped, Jake left his office and headed back toward the holding area.

Kelly slipped back into his office and grabbed the frame from his desk. Flipping it over, she loosened several metal clips to release the back. Beneath a sliver of cardboard the print on the photography paper was clear. *Agfa.* Identical to the shot left in her house.

I only use Fuji. Miller's words echoed through her mind.

Kelly squeezed her eyes shut and took a steadying breath. She glanced again at the photo. Jake's reasons for not helping their investigation were becoming a whole lot clearer.

Either she was about to jump to the worst conclusion of her life, or she and Dan had been focused on the wrong person the entire time.

A glimmer of cellophane caught her eye and she picked up the empty candy wrapper she'd left discarded on the edge of Jake's desk. Jolly Roger. The same wrapper she'd found beneath Rachel's desk after the threatening photo had been left.

The Candy Man. Could it be?

She began to tremble, gripping the desk's edge to steady herself. She had to hold it together, had to find Dan.

Kelly replaced the back of the frame, leaving it facedown on the desk. She slid the photo into her backpack, and raced for the exit, frantically punching Dan's number into her cell phone as she ran.

DAN PUNCHED OFF the power on his cell phone as he stepped into Helen's room. A nurse looked up from taking vital signs. Kelly was nowhere in sight.

"I was hoping to find Kelly Weir here." He hid his disappointment.

"She called earlier," the nurse answered. "I told her Helen was breathing on her own, but still unconscious. She said she'd be in a bit later."

"Thanks." He pulled a chair close to Helen. The woman's color had improved and the sight of her face free of the ventilator tube brought a smile to his lips.

"She did mention she was going to stop by the police station on her way in," the nurse offered.

Dan frowned. Why? To see Jake? To see Miller? He hadn't even had a chance to tell her Miller was dead, and Jake hadn't mentioned anything about expecting Kelly to stop by.

Helen moaned and Dan jumped to his feet.

"Helen," the nurse cooed softly. "You coming back to us?"

Helen's pale lids fluttered open then closed again.

Dan's heart lodged in his throat. He fought to keep his emotions—and hope—controlled.

Her eyes opened again. Dan's heart twisted at the sight of their faded blue color. He bent to hold her hand, pressing his lips into her weathered flesh.

"Hello, gorgeous." Relief blurred his vision.

Helen's lips parted and she struggled to speak. No sound was audible.

"You're dry, honey." The nurse moved toward her supply tray. "Let me swab out your mouth."

"You'll be happy to know Miller's been arrested," Dan spoke carefully. No need to tell her of Miller's death just yet. "He'll never hurt you again."

Helen's eyes darted wildly from side to side as the nurse rubbed the damp foam swab along her lips and into her mouth.

Dan didn't understand her reaction, but dread began to puddle in his gut just the same.

"Miller attacked you, right?" His throat tightened. He mentally scolded himself. *Of course* Miller had attacked her.

Helen shook her head, and Dan fought to hide the surprise and fear seeping through him.

"Miller didn't attack you?"

She shook her head again and winced.

"Take it easy on the movement," the nurse said. "Try to speak."

"Who attacked you, Helen?" Dan's heart jackhammered against his ribs. "Try to tell me."

Her lips moved again, but nothing more than a

whisper sounded. The nurse bent close, listening intently, wrinkles creasing her forehead.

She looked up at Dan. "That's odd."

"What?" Dan leaned in, frantic to know what Helen had said.

"I think she's saying Arnold." The nurse looked dazed. "She can't mean Detective Arnold, can she?"

Dan didn't stick around to answer. He hit the hall in a full sprint. Suddenly the pieces all fit. The reluctance to help. Miller's unexpected death. Jake's back pain. The pills.

Arnold. *The Candy Man.*

Kelly had walked into the office of a killer.

JAKE WATCHED from the opposite end of the hall until Kelly left his office. Once her footfalls faded away, he stepped into his office and closed the door.

The frame lay facedown on top of his desk. He reached for it with a steady hand and turned it over. Empty. Damn the girl. She wasn't as stupid as he thought.

He picked up the phone and punched the intercom to the duty desk. "I'm headed out for a bit. Something I need to take care of."

He tossed the frame into the trashcan, closed his eyes and took a deep, slow breath. Another piece. He should have killed her when he'd had the chance at the cemetery.

He hurried down the steps to the parking lot, doing his best to remain calm. After all, there was no need to rush.

He knew exactly where to find her.

Chapter Fifteen

Kelly patted Maddie's cheek, praying the woman would wake up.

The attending aide spoke softly. "She had a bad night, hon."

"I understand." Panic rose in Kelly's throat. She had to know the truth—had to know if Maddie had seen Rachel's death.

The aide offered a kind smile then left the room.

Kelly closed her eyes. My God. Poor Maddie had been telling the truth all along, and no one had listened.

"He'll kill you," a voice whispered.

Kelly opened her eyes, focusing her gaze on Dan's mother.

"Don't be sad." Maddie's pale stare appeared more frightened than usual. "You've got to leave now."

"Shh." Kelly held the older woman's hand, hoping to calm her. "I know you saw Rachel die. I believe you."

"No one believes me. Won't let me tell you."

Maddie's gaze never left Kelly's face, yet she seemed to drift away, fading before Kelly's eyes.

"I'm right here." Kelly leaned close, urging Dan's mother to stay with her—to stay focused. Her pulse pounded in her ears. "Tell me now, Maddie. Tell me."

"He killed you."

"Who killed Rachel? You saw it, didn't you?"

"The Candy Man." Maddie's eyelids fluttered closed.

Ice raced down Kelly's spine, and she bit back a curse. It had been Jake all along. She and Dan had been so far off course.

"Maddie." Kelly gripped the tiny woman's shoulders and squeezed. "Who's the Candy Man? Please. I need to hear you say it."

Maddie's eyes opened, growing wide and filling with tears. Kelly suddenly felt a presence behind her. Standing close. A tremor ripped through her body.

"Too late," Maddie whispered.

A hand gripped Kelly's shoulder. Fear squeezed her heart, and she struggled to breath.

"Meet the Candy Man." Jake's voice resonated firm and clear. "Isn't that right, Maddie?"

Kelly's knees buckled. Jake moved quickly, gripping her firmly by the waist.

"Whoa, there. Don't faint before you hear the whole story." He turned Kelly to face him, his eyes ice-cold, his features set like stone. "That is why you've hung in there this long, isn't it? You wanted to know what happened to Rachel?"

He leaned forward, his sweet breath brushing over Kelly's face. "Guess what, little Kelly? You're going to experience just what Rachel did. Firsthand."

"Why?" She forced the word through her paralyzed throat.

"A better question would be why not." Jake leaned to pat Maddie's arm. "How you doing today, Maddie? Still hallucinating?"

The old woman visibly trembled. Kelly hated Jake for scaring her. For killing Rachel. For lying to them all.

He turned to Kelly and scowled. "You and I are going to take a walk." He pointed toward the door. "You're going to go very quietly with me down that hall."

He moved closer, his face a mere fraction of an inch from hers. "You wouldn't want anything to happen to Dan's mother, would you? After all, she'll be all he's got left after you're dead."

Kelly's insides twisted. She struggled to think, raw fear pressing heavy against her. There had to be a way to reason with Jake—a way out of this nightmare.

He glared at her, laughing. The sound sent shivers tumbling through her body.

"I can see the wheels turning. No getting out of it, sweetheart. Sorry." He linked his arm through hers, leading her toward the open door. "You've been fun to play with, though. Kind of disappointed it took you this long to figure it out. Think Rachel might have been a bit quicker."

They passed an aide in the hall. The woman smiled and spoke to Jake. "Here to see Maddie?"

Jake nodded in return. "Yes, and I ran into an old friend." He tightened his grip. "We're headed out for a late lunch."

"Have fun." The woman brightened as she hurried away, obviously intent on her work, not noticing the death grip Jake had on Kelly's arm.

"How do I know you won't hurt her?" Dan's mother would be at this madman's mercy. The thought terrified her.

He chuckled. "Please. They haven't believed her so far. Why would they start now?"

Kelly glanced over her shoulder at the aide's back and thought about screaming, but she couldn't risk Maddie's safety. Panic seized her as Jake pushed open the exit door, jerking her toward the marsh.

Where on earth was Dan? Hadn't he gotten her message? *Hurry,* she prayed. *Hurry.*

DAN RACED OUT of the hospital parking lot, pulling his cell phone from his pocket. He had to reach Kelly before it was too late.

The message indicator chirped as he powered on the phone. He punched in the code to retrieve the call as he kicked the car into gear, peeling out of the parking lot.

"Jake's behind it all. I think he killed Miller." Kelly's voice sounded frantic and rushed. "I'm going to your mother's. She was right, Dan. *She was right.* I think she did see him kill Rachel. Jake's the Candy Man." There was a beat of silence. "What have we done?"

Dan slammed on the brakes, yanking the wheel

in the opposite direction. The tires squealed, the stench of burnt rubber instant. He depressed the clutch and shifted. Hard.

Adrenaline poured through him, flooding him with the hyperawareness that Kelly's life depended on him. He'd failed Rachel because of a missed message. He would not let Kelly suffer the same fate.

JAKE'S FINGERS dug into the flesh of Kelly's upper arm. She fought the urge to cry out in fear and pain, refusing to give him the satisfaction.

"You fooled us. We thought Miller was behind the whole thing."

"Idiots." He forced her forward. "Shut up and walk."

"I didn't give you enough credit, Jake. I thought you plain didn't care. I never imagined you were ignoring our investigation in order to protect yourself."

He yanked her around to face him. His face twisted with rage and urgency.

"You're quite brilliant," she continued, hoping her words might slow him down. She had to stall, had to give Dan time. Cold fear washed through her veins, but she willed her mind to stay calm. To think.

Jake's features relaxed and a smirk pulled at the corner of his mouth. One eyebrow arched. "That's what I've been trying to tell everyone."

Keep him talking, Kelly thought. Keep him talking until Dan can get here.

"How did you do it? You had the doctor to involve and the prescriptions to fill. That doesn't even include the kids running the pills to different schools." She shook her head. "How many campuses did you work?"

"Fourteen."

Kelly's mind went momentarily blank from shock. *Fourteen.* She and Dan never dreamed the drug ring had been so large. How many lives had he damaged—or ruined?

She forced a laugh, amazed she could even manage the sound through her panic. "You must be rich."

"Very. And no one is going to take that away from me. Not you." He leaned close and she flinched. "And not your boyfriend."

He pulled on her arm and they resumed their trudge toward the water.

"I didn't know there were that many schools in this area." The words came in a rush, a feeble attempt to slow down their forward progress.

"Too many questions. Shut up and walk."

DAN BURST into his mother's room. Terror filled her wide eyes, and tear tracks streaked her pale face. A nurse stood poised to give her a shot. Dan yelled out, "Don't sedate her."

"But, Mr. Steele," the woman argued. "She's completely irrational."

Dan rushed to his mother's side, cupping her face in his palms. "I don't think so. I think she's been telling us the truth all along."

"He took her," Maddie whispered. "You're too late."

Frustration and fear seized Dan's heart, but he forced himself to stay calm. He had to—for Kelly.

"Who took her, Momma? Who took Kelly?"

"The Candy Man," Maddie whispered.

"See?" the nurse said. "I told you she was at it again."

"Shut up," Dan snapped. "Let her speak."

"Well, I—"

Dan shot the nurse a glare, freezing her words on her lips.

"I'll be in the hall if you need me." She recapped the syringe, stepping quickly out of the room.

"Momma," Dan urged. "Was Kelly here?"

"Rachel."

He shook his head, wincing. "No. Not Rachel. Rachel's dead." He looked directly into his mother's eyes, hope building as they sparked to life. "Kelly. Was my friend Kelly here?"

"He took her." Her voice rang out strong and sharp.

"Who did?"

"The detective. The Candy Man."

Dan's heart sank to his stomach. "When?" His extremities tingled with the faded effects of his adrenaline rush.

"Not long." She narrowed her eyes. "You have to hurry, Danny. He took her for a walk."

"The marsh? Does he walk in the marsh?"

Maddie nodded. "Have to hurry."

Dan kissed her forehead before he ran down the hall to the activities room. He leaned against the plate-glass window, scrutinizing the foliage below. Deep and dark, it offered no view of Kelly or Jake.

How would he ever find them in the tangle of weeds and evergreens?

A shadow moved and he focused, squinting for a better image. A tree branch swung wildly, and his breath whooshed from his lungs. Nothing. Probably a bird taking flight.

The long afternoon sun appeared from behind a bank of clouds sending slashes of light filtering through to the marsh below. There. A flash of red. Another. Kelly's hair.

Kelly and Jake were headed toward the water and she was still on her feet. Dan dashed for the hall, knocking an aide against the wall in his rush.

"Sorry!" he yelled over his shoulder as he slipped on the tile floor, righted himself and raced for the exit.

He wasn't too late. Kelly was alive. Dan planned to do whatever it took to make sure she stayed that way.

SUNLIGHT STREAKED through the trees. Light reflected off of the sound, ratcheting up Kelly's dread. They were close to the water. Too close.

She had to stop Jake, had to stall.

"Jake, I really want to know how you did it. I'll never be able to tell anyone."

Jake turned, pinning her with his emotionless stare, his gaze frigid.

"Please." Kelly forced the word, hating to ask this madman for anything. "Dan and I worked so hard. At least tell me how you did it."

For several seconds only the sounds of the marsh filled the air between them.

"It was a matter of control." Jake's words came slowly.

Good, she thought. Keep talking. *Take your time.*

"Control and owed favors," he continued. "It's what makes the world go around."

Kelly shuddered at the harshness of his tone but nodded, urging him to go on.

"Our Dr. Robinson had a few DUI charges under his belt. Our residents don't like that, especially not when his last offense was a hit-and-run. I kept it quiet, and I kept him out of jail. He kept me in prescriptions."

Kelly nodded. "And Miller came here with a track record of sexual harassment and stalking from New Jersey."

"And I kept it under wraps." Pride danced in his eyes. "Our small-town folks wouldn't have liked knowing he settled near their daughters. I made sure they never found out."

"And he stocked the Oxygesic?"

"A win-win for us all." Jake laughed. "The institute made the prescriptions look legitimate, and Miller's records backed them up. I made sure he made enough from the transactions to keep him quiet. After all, he needed me in order for him to exist in this town."

"And the kids?"

Jake shook his head as if he impressed himself. "The easiest part." He tipped his head, clucking his tongue. "Do you have any idea how many college kids flock here during spring break or senior week?"

Kelly shook her head. His calculated words made her feel sick. She fought the bile clawing its way up her throat.

"Thousands," Jake answered. "Underage drinking. Drunk and disorderly. Driving under the influence. Speeding. Reckless endangerment."

When he leveled his gaze at her once more, his eyes glittered with amusement.

"So many kids doing so many illegal things and so grateful to keep their mishaps quiet. Trust me." He puffed out his chest. "They'd much rather run a few pills for me than have Mommy, Daddy and their college find out what they'd done."

He leaned close and Kelly fought the urge to gag.

"They all happily made their pickups and drop-offs when I dictated. Fourteen schools. Major colleges and universities, community campuses, high schools, you name it."

High schools. Anger tangled with the terror growing inside Kelly.

"No one caught on for a long time." Jake gestured widely with his free arm. "I ruled from here to Norfolk to Williamsburg to Richmond. I ran it all."

"What happened?"

"Diane snooped. She found my hidden profits and started asking questions. Lots of questions."

Tears welled in Kelly's eyes. "And you killed her?"

Jake pursed his lip, as if remembering. "Feisty girl. She fought it."

"But you loved her. How could you kill her?"

His expression fell slack, his voice monotone. "Love is an illusion, Kelly. She would have turned me in. I didn't have a choice."

"And Rachel?"

Jake's eyes narrowed. He rubbed his chin as if for effect. "Rachel was bright. Brighter than I gave her credit for. She found some of my ledgers."

"And hid them in a book."

His grip tightened painfully on her arm. He yanked her close. "How did you know that?"

"I have them."

Jake's lips pinched into a thin line, anger seething from his glare. "Where?"

Kelly shook her head. "Where they can be found."

She had left the backpack in her car. Even if Jake succeeded in killing her, she prayed someone would get there before he did.

He grasped her shoulders and shook her. She flinched, turning away her face.

"Look at me." His words resonated with desperation. "I need those notes. Where are they?"

"I hid them."

He slapped her, and she fell to the ground. Tears stung her eyes but she scrambled to get to her feet. To run.

"You little—"

He dropped on top of her, pinning her down. Leaves and pine needles tore into her face and filled her mouth. He shoved something between her lips, forcing her teeth apart with his fingers.

"Chew."

She sputtered, fighting the bitter taste and coughing as his hands tightened around her throat. His fingers slowly choked off her air supply.

Kelly cheeked the pill he'd forced on her and fought to speak. "If you kill me, you'll never find the notes."

"I'll find them." His tone had grown confident and calm, as if her struggle soothed him. "I'll find them because I'm smarter than you. I'm smarter than Steele."

"No, you're not."

He increased the pressure on her throat. Kelly's vision dimmed.

"I'm a detective, sweetheart. Let's do some detective work. You must have just found them, or you wouldn't have been chasing Miller all of this time. I'd say they're on your dining room table or in that backpack you've always got with you."

He frowned. Kelly struggled against him but he was too strong. She clawed at his face, but he dodged her fingernails and squeezed tighter.

Her vision wavered. She felt herself slipping away, fading. She had to fight. Had to survive. For Dan. For Maddie. For Rachel.

"I know." Jake moved his face close to hers, whispering. "You had your backpack when you came to see me. You were going to tell me then, but you realized I was the one who took the picture. I'll just pull your little backpack out of your car after I dump your body in the sound."

He laughed but his voice was growing detached—fading. Kelly couldn't understand. Couldn't think.

"Kelly."

Who was calling her?

"Hold on."

Dan. He'd made it.

His voice was the last thing she heard as she slipped into unconsciousness.

A BRANCH WHIPPED against Dan's cheek but he pushed through the pain, running fast. He had to find Kelly and Jake. Had to locate them before it was too late.

He paused for a moment and listened, praying for a voice, a sound, anything to guide him through the dense foliage.

Nothing.

He set off once more, desperately hoping he was headed in the right direction. That's when he heard them.

Laughter. Jake's laughter. He'd know the sound anywhere.

Dan stopped for a split second to center on the sound. It was Jake's voice, talking, murmuring.

"Kelly," Dan yelled. He had to let her know he'd save her. "Hang on!"

He raced toward the sound of Jake's voice. Horror gripped him when Jake and Kelly came into sight. She lay sprawled on the ground—hair splayed over leaves and pine needles, eyes closed, body limp. Jake hovered over her, his hands clenched like a vise on her slender throat.

"No." Dan hurled himself at Jake, breaking his hold on Kelly and slamming his body to the ground. Jake rolled, freeing himself from beneath Dan's weight.

"You're too late, Romeo."

The words sent a series of tremors through Dan's body. He stole a glance at Kelly. No sign of movement. No sign of life.

"No," he whispered. "Not Kelly."

Dan pulled himself to his knees to move toward her. Jake hit him full-force from behind, slamming him face-first into the dirt.

He struggled, fighting with every ounce of his strength. He couldn't let Jake win. Not this time. The two grappled for position, rolling in a frenzied tangle of arms and legs. They slammed into Kelly's body then careened in the opposite direction.

For a brief moment, Dan lay pinned, back to the ground. He struggled to pull in a breath, forcing his gaze to Kelly. Her chest heaved. Her eyelashes fluttered and she coughed. His heart soared. *Alive.* She was alive.

He fought with renewed fury. He had to wrestle Jake away from her to give her time to recover. Time to escape.

He slammed his foot against the hard ground, using the leverage to ram his knee into Jake's groin. Jake moaned and rolled to his side. Dan wrapped his arms around Jake's waist and they hurtled together, farther away from Kelly.

Jake slipped from Dan's hold, scrambling to his feet and circling. Dan circled backward, trying to anticipate Jake's next move.

"It's over," Dan sputtered. "You'll never get away with another murder. Let alone two."

Jake rushed and his fist connected with Dan's lip. Dan spit out the metallic taste of blood, dodging the second blow and hurling himself at Jake's waist.

Jake's back slammed against the gnarled trunk of a tree. His head bounced off the bark and his eyes dulled momentarily before he howled like a wounded animal and plowed Dan backward onto the ground.

"You're just one more piece," Jake muttered. "One more piece of the damn puzzle. You and the girl. Then no one will be able to touch me."

Dan forced Jake into a roll, pinning him against the dirt.

"Don't you think someone in your department will catch on?" Dan's words spattered blood onto Jake's face.

"They're too stupid," Jake snarled. "Too stupid. Like you."

"Was it worth it Jake? Diane? Rachel? How many others did you kill?"

"They were going to take it all away." Jake's hand snaked out, searching for a weapon and anchoring on a large rock. "Soon I'll have everything I ever wanted."

Dan struggled to block Jake's hand, now wielding the rock. "What? Money? Take your money and leave. Leave now."

Jake grimaced and swung at Dan. The blow glanced off Dan's temple. Pain exploded, spreading down the side of his face. Jake slipped free of his grip, clambering to his feet, arms at the defensive.

They moved in a slow waltz. One around the other.

Where was Kelly? Had she gotten away? Dan couldn't risk a look. Couldn't lose control. He only hoped she was far away. Safe from Jake and his insanity.

"Enough." Jake dropped the rock to the ground, pulling a pistol from an ankle holster.

Dan's pulse rapped a staccato beat in his ears, his breath coming in ragged gasps.

"I didn't want to use this." Jake shrugged. "The noise. You know? But I don't see where you leave me much choice."

A flash of color moved among the trees behind Jake. Kelly. Dan fought the urge to look at her, focusing his gaze on Jake. He had to keep Jake's attention and gun on him. Not Kelly.

It took every ounce of effort Dan had left to hold a poker face and pray. Pray that Kelly had seen the gun and would make her move in time.

PAIN RIPPED through every inch of Kelly's body, her throat bruised and bleeding. A biting, bitter taste filled her mouth. The pill had partially dissolved before she could spit it out. She could only hope it had been Oxygesic and nothing even more lethal.

She stepped from behind one large tree trunk, quickly ducking behind another, working her way closer to where Dan and Jake struggled.

There. A flicker of recognition in Dan's eyes. Had he seen her? If only he could hang on.

Kelly saw Jake slip the gun from his ankle, but not before he tossed the rock. It rolled a few feet short of where she hid. She needed a weapon and the rock would have to do.

"You're no better than me, you know," Jake said, keeping the gun trained on Dan's face. "You're just as guilty." Jake's laughter rang through the marsh. "Hell. You live in the biggest house around with the money you made from Oxygesic. At least I stayed humble."

Stall him, Kelly silently urged Dan. Keep him talking.

"How do you sleep at night?" Dan asked. "Look at the countless lives you've ruined."

Jake lowered the gun for a split second and cackled. The sound steeled Kelly's determination. No way would she let this madman win.

"It's easy," Jake answered Dan's question. "I take an Oxygesic."

Kelly seized the moment. She plucked the rock from the ground and hurled it underhanded straight for the back of Jake's head, never taking her eyes from her target. It impacted with a thud, missing its target, but slamming just between Jake's shoulder blades. He staggered.

Dan seized the opportunity, tackling Jake to the ground. The gun skittered across pine needles and leaves.

Kelly held her breath as Dan fought, landing a fist to Jake's jaw. The blow connected solidly, rendering Jake limp—unconscious at last.

Dan plucked the gun from the ground next to Jake, checking his body for other weapons. Finding none, his gaze lifted to Kelly.

Sobs racked her body, tears spilling over her lashes as Dan reached her, enfolding her in his arms.

"It's over." His warm breath brushed her damp cheeks.

He held her at arm's length, his eyes bright with emotion, admiration and incredulity. "You saved my life."

"No." Kelly felt her strength fade as the rush of adrenaline slipped from her body. "You saved mine."

He pulled her close, whispering against her ear, "Maybe we saved each other."

"DIANE AND RACHEL." Sadness tinged Dan's words. "Dead for no reason other than money."

Kelly's heart ached for all he'd lost. He pulled a blanket tight around her shoulders, and she settled close, watching as the paramedics took Jake away, handcuffed to a backboard.

"Greed," she uttered the word flatly. "They're dead because of his greed."

"I wish our company had never developed that drug."

The regret in Dan's voice filled her with the desire to soothe him, comfort him, help him heal. "No. You've helped millions."

She leaned against his shoulder, stealing a glimpse of the bruised line of his strong jaw, the rumpled disarray of his dark brown waves. Awareness danced along her every nerve ending.

She knew without a doubt in her heart she loved him. Completely.

"How's your poor head?" She forced the words through a throat choked with raw emotion and need.

"Paramedic said I'm fine. Scrapes and bruises." Concern deepened the fine lines around his eyes. "How about your throat?"

"They wanted to take me in." She gave him a weak smile. "I said no."

"God only knows what he gave you."

"You and I both know what it was. That's how he managed the positive tox screens for Diane and Rachel." She watched his expression hopefully. "I'm not allowed to spend the night alone. Any ideas?"

His gaze softened, sending heat flooding through her. "A few." His eyes blazed, and she sighed.

"Dan?" She shifted closer, savoring the warmth of his hold on her, wishing he'd never let go.

"Hmm?" He moved against her, pressing his cheek to hers.

"Jake said he thought love was only an illusion."

"I think Jake's a fool."

Kelly's stomach caught, tightening at the sure timbre of his voice.

"How about you? You agree with him?"

"Not anymore," she whispered, suddenly very sure Jake had been wrong about everything. "Not anymore."

Epilogue

Several days later, Kelly stood at the ocean's edge. The cool surf brushed the tips of her bare toes and she fingered Rachel's gold locket, now hanging proudly at the hollow of her throat.

The crime-scene team had found the heirloom in the marsh near where Jake had attacked Kelly. Rachel's brother had insisted Kelly keep it as a symbol of the friendship she and Rachel had shared.

She'd come to terms with the way that friendship had ended, knowing deep in her heart Rachel would have forgiven her stubbornness, just as she'd forgiven herself.

A gull swooped past—low and silent over the dark ocean swells. Kelly wrapped her arms around her waist, smiling up at the sun as it peeked from between heavy clouds.

It was funny where life took you when you weren't looking. Life had brought her here. Brought her to Dan and shown her a way to trust in love again.

Kelly turned and headed back toward the street.

Helen would have her head if she was late for dinner. The feisty woman had insisted on having a cookout to prove how well she felt.

It had been days since she and Dan had survived Jake's attack, having agreed to take the time apart to heal and think. Her insides tilted, nervous energy building at the idea of seeing him again at Helen's. Kelly had come to a decision about her future—never more sure of anything. She only hoped he'd feel the same way.

A half hour later, wondering where Dan was, Kelly listened to Helen's excited chatter.

"And then he put the poison in a meatball sandwich," Helen said as she slapped burgers onto the grill.

Kelly shook her head, glancing at the woman with a smile. Even after her brush with death, Helen sounded like a schoolgirl as she recounted the details.

Helen turned and headed back toward the door, the red bandana around her head flapping in the breeze. "I'm going in for a cold one. How about you?"

Kelly smiled, wrinkling her nose. "I'm okay. But, thanks. Hey," she yelled after Helen, "I thought the doctor said no alcohol for a while."

Helen gave a dismissive wave of her hand. "Doctor. Shmocter."

Kelly looked to the sky. "You're hopeless."

"Where's that boyfriend of yours?" Helen hollered. "He'd better not make me burn my burgers."

Dan waited for Helen to step back into the house before he approached Kelly.

She sat in one of Helen's purple plastic chairs with Edgar snuggled into her lap. He noticed the gleam of gold at her neck and realized she must be wearing Rachel's locket. He hoped she'd finally forgiven herself, as he'd forgiven himself.

His sister had died trying to stop Arnold's crime. She'd died a hero, not a victim. He'd honor her memory by working to stop additional abuse and by letting love into his own life. If Kelly could find a way to love him.

"Hey," he spoke softly as he approached.

Kelly turned to face him, a warm, pink flush lighting her face. "I've been wondering when you'd show up."

He sank to the ground next to her, reaching up to scratch the top of Edgar's head. "You finished packing?"

She nodded.

"When are you leaving?"

"Well—" she looked to the sky "—that depends on you."

His pulse accelerated as he stared at her. "What do you mean?"

"I'd like you to meet my family while we're up that way. Before I move down here and all."

Dan's mouth fell open.

She looked at him then laughed, her eyes sparkling with delight.

"I've rendered you speechless." She brushed her fingertip across his cheek. "I didn't think that possible."

"I love you, Kelly." He'd never meant the words

as deeply as he meant them now, looking into her eyes.

"I know you do." She grinned. "I love you, too."

She stroked Edgar and stared out into the yard. "I spoke with Frank Healey. He's arranged for me to continue renting Rachel's house." She nodded. "I think I'll like it here in Summer Shores. It's quiet. Uneventful."

Dan grinned, pulling himself to his feet then hoisting Kelly to hers. He wrapped her tightly in his arms. Edgar yowled in protest but clung to Kelly's shoulder.

"So." Kelly gave him a seductive smile. "Would you mind if I hung around?"

"Mind? I can't imagine life without you." He searched her face, hope rising in his chest. "You should hang around forever."

Tears glistened in Kelly's eyes and she nodded. "I like the way you think."

Dan covered her mouth with his, savoring the taste of his future. Their future. Together.

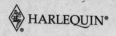

HARLEQUIN®

INTRIGUE®

**Has a brand-new trilogy
to keep you
on the edge of your seat!**

Better than all the rest...

THE ENFORCERS

BY

DEBRA WEBB

JOHN DOE ON HER DOORSTEP

April

EXECUTIVE BODYGUARD

May

MAN OF HER DREAMS

June

Available wherever Harlequin Books are sold.

www.eHarlequin.com

HIMOHD

SPOTLIGHT

National bestselling author

JOANNA WAYNE

The Gentlemen's Club

A homicide in the French Quarter of New Orleans has attorney Rachel Powers obsessed with finding the killer. As she investigates, she is shocked to discover that some of the Big Easy's most respected gentlemen will go to any lengths to satisfy their darkest sexual desires. Even murder.

*A gripping new novel...
coming in June.*

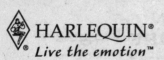

Live the emotion™

**Bonus Features,
including:**

**Author Interview,
Romance—
New Orleans Style,
and Bonus Read!**

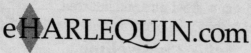

If you enjoyed what you just read,
then we've got an offer you can't resist!

Take 2 bestselling love stories FREE!

Plus get a FREE surprise gift!

Clip this page and mail it to Harlequin Reader Service®

IN U.S.A.
3010 Walden Ave.
P.O. Box 1867
Buffalo, N.Y. 14240-1867

IN CANADA
P.O. Box 609
Fort Erie, Ontario
L2A 5X3

YES! Please send me 2 free Harlequin Intrigue® novels and my free surprise gift. After receiving them, if I don't wish to receive anymore, I can return the shipping statement marked cancel. If I don't cancel, I will receive 4 brand-new novels each month, before they're available in stores! In the U.S.A., bill me at the bargain price of $4.24 plus 25¢ shipping and handling per book and applicable sales tax, if any*. In Canada, bill me at the bargain price of $4.99 plus 25¢ shipping and handling per book and applicable taxes**. That's the complete price and a savings of at least 10% off the cover prices—what a great deal! I understand that accepting the 2 free books and gift places me under no obligation ever to buy any books. I can always return a shipment and cancel at any time. Even if I never buy another book from Harlequin, the 2 free books and gift are mine to keep forever.

181 HDN DZ7N
381 HDN DZ7P

Name	(PLEASE PRINT)	
Address	Apt.#	
City	State/Prov.	Zip/Postal Code

Not valid to current Harlequin Intrigue® subscribers.

Want to try two free books from another series?
Call 1-800-873-8635 or visit www.morefreebooks.com.

* Terms and prices subject to change without notice. Sales tax applicable in N.Y.
** Canadian residents will be charged applicable provincial taxes and GST.
   All orders subject to approval. Offer limited to one per household.
   ® are registered trademarks owned and used by the trademark owner and or its licensee.

INT04R
©2004 Harlequin Enterprises Limited

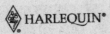